Captain Cobwebb and the Red Transistor

This Armada book belongs to:

BOB BRASS

12 FLORA DR

MTP 1A2

759-7260

Captain Cobwebb And The Red Transistor

Gordon Boshell

Illustrated by Graham Thompson

Armada

First published in 1974 by
Macdonald & Co. (Publishers), Ltd.

This edition first published in
Armada in 1978 by Fontana Paperbacks,
14 St. James's Place,
London SW1A 1PF

© Gordon Boshell 1974

Printed in Great Britain
by Love & Malcomson Ltd.,
Brighton Road, Redhill,
Surrey.

CONDITIONS OF SALE:
This book is sold subject to the condition that
it shall not, by way of trade or otherwise, be lent,
re-sold, hired out or otherwise circulated without
the publisher's prior consent in any form of
binding or cover other than that in which it is
published and without a similar condition
including this condition being imposed on the
subsequent purchaser.

CONTENTS

CHAPTER 1

A MYSTERIOUS BROADCAST

IT really was most unusual. There were Mr. and Mrs. Green and their two sons, David and Toby, all together in the same room, yet it was so quiet that you could have heard a pin drop. As a rule, either David would be making a noise, or Toby, or they would both be making a noise and this always meant that Mr. Green or Mrs. Green, or Mr. and Mrs. Green together, would also be making a noise calling to David or Toby, or both, telling them to *stop* making a noise.

But tonight, no. All was peace and quiet. Outdoors the moon sailed in a cloudless sky and it was bitterly cold. Inside the fire burned bright. Mr. Green toasted his toes and tried to solve the crossword puzzle in the evening paper. Mrs. Green sat knitting and thinking about the new wardrobe she had just put in the boys' bedroom and how the extra space would enable her to make that room tidy at last—by which she meant getting all their clothing into the wardrobe and stuffing the chest of drawers with the comics, books, games, roller-skates, cowboy pistols and catapults that David and Toby preferred to leave scattered over the floor (where, as every boy knows, it's much easier to find a thing when you want it).

In fact, both David and Toby like to be on the floor themselves, and that's where they were at this moment. Toby had his comic spread out on the carpet and was reading *The Mad Scientist's Revenge*, slipping his hand into his jacket pocket from time to time to pull out a liquorice allsort—quietly, of course, so that David wouldn't notice and ask him for one.

David was quite absorbed in putting together *The Young Constructor's Easibild Transistor Radio* and he'd very nearly got all the pieces assembled when suddenly the peaceful silence was shattered.

'Oh, NO!' said David, very loudly and crossly. And right at that moment Mr. Green exploded: 'This is the silliest, most idiotic crossword clue I've ever seen!'

All this sudden noise made Toby jump so much that his hand slipped and he tore his comic right across.

'Now look what you've made me do!' he shouted, jumping up and waving the torn pieces in the air.

'Boys, boys!' said Mrs. Green sharply, for the uproar had so startled her that she had dropped a couple of stitches in her knitting. 'Stop quarrelling at once!'

'I wasn't quarrelling,' said Toby sulkily. 'It was all . . .'

'. . . all somebody else's fault, I'll be bound,' said Mr. Green as if *he* had had nothing to do with the affair. 'I knew it was too much to hope that I'd get one complete evening of peace and quiet . . .'

Mrs. Green could see real trouble ahead and she acted at once before Mr. Green could say anything further. 'I'm sure we're all sorry your comic got torn, Toby,' she said soothingly, 'but there's some transparent sticky tape in the top drawer of the sideboard, so you can soon mend it. And you, David, what's the matter?'

'There's only one piece needed to finish my transistor radio,' grumbled David, 'and the one that's left in the box is the wrong one.'

'Well, don't give in yet,' said Mrs. Green. 'Go over it again and if you find it won't work then we'll take it back to the shop and get it changed.'

Toby could understand how fed up David must be feeling so he said: 'I'll read the instructions aloud while you check each point, David, then you won't have to keep turning from one thing to the other. How about that?' And David, feeling a whole lot better, agreed.

Mrs. Green said: 'And I suggest you boys take all your things up to your bedroom, so you won't disturb your father, because he has a very difficult crossword puzzle to do. Put yourselves to bed when you've finished.'

As they were leaving the room to go upstairs, Mrs. Green smiled fondly at Mr. Green and said: 'And now, while the boys are solving their problems, perhaps we can solve yours, Walter?'

Mr. Green shook his paper irritably. 'Their problems are child's play compared to mine,' he said. 'I defy anyone to make head or tail of this utterly ridiculous clue. It's a word of eight letters and the clue is *Ernie, canonised, is as unrelenting as can be.* Now, what on earth is anyone supposed to make of that?'

'Oh, it's easy!' said David, pausing at the door. Mr.

Green glared at him angrily and Mrs. Green began to feel worried again.

'Ernie is short for Ernest,' said David. 'When a man is canonised he becomes a saint—so that makes him *Saint* Ernest. But we shorten the word "saint" into "St.", so that gives us the word S T E R N E S T. The most unrelenting man, in eight letters, is the sternest, see?'

'Why, ye-es. Yes, indeed,' said Mr. Green. 'Quite so. Thank you, my boy.'

'Don't mention it,' answered a voice from halfway up the stairs. Mr. Green bent over his crossword puzzle, Mrs. Green smiled and started picking up her dropped stitches. Peace had returned.

In their bedroom David and Toby went carefully through all the instructions for building the transistor radio set. All the parts were grouped in different colours and the places on the baseboard where they were to go were coloured also. Blue parts fitted into the blue plugs, yellow into yellow, black into black. All these were in their right places and one plug alone remained to be filled. It was coloured green. Only one transistor remained to be plugged in. It was coloured red. There was no mention of a red transistor in the instructions.

David looked glum. 'I told you it was wrong,' he said.

Toby pondered. 'Perhaps somebody forgot and dabbed the wrong colour on that piece,' he said. 'Will it fit in the holes?'

'Yes, it'll fit in there,' said David. 'But suppose I put it in and it's wrong and the whole thing busts up? The shopman won't change it then.'

'I don't think there's enough power in a couple of flashlight batteries to make *anything* blow up,' Toby said. 'I think that if that piece is the wrong one the set just won't work at all.'

David thought this over for a while and made his mind up.

'All right. Here goes.' He plugged in the red transistor, clipped the box top over the baseboard and screwed the dial and pointer into place.

'Now listen,' he said, and flipped over the switch at the side of the box.

Nothing happened.

'Turn the dial,' said Toby. 'Very slowly.'

The pointer moved from 0 towards 1. Suddenly there was a crackle, then a faint hissing sound.

'Well, there's current passing through the loud-speaker, anyway,' said David, relieved. Slowly, very, very slowly, he moved the pointer round the dial. The hissing became a little louder. Then there was a burst of crackling and David exclaimed: 'I can hear somebody speaking!'

'Can't you get rid of that crackling?'

'I'll try. No. It's no use. Come closer. Perhaps we can make some sense of this between us.'

The boys pressed their ears close to the loud-speaker. The crackling came in great surges, now loud, now soft. 'There it is!' whispered David. 'Listen!'

Faintly, but clearly, they heard a voice say: *'Brothers of the High Council of Grunia. Our land is being attacked . . .'* Then the crackling surged up again.

'Where's Grunia?' demanded Toby.

'Shut up! Listen! Here it comes again . . .'

'. . . . . undeclared war,' said the voice. And then . . . *'everywhere the Wurgs . . . . ., ...'*

CRACKLE . . CRACKLE . . CRACKLE.

'Call Brindor . . . make announcement . . . Folk of Grunia . . . . . Bid him tell them to . . . . .'

And there, suddenly, the voice ended. The crackling died down, and though a faint hissing continued at that point on the dial, it proved impossible to pick up any more information about the mysterious war and the equally mysterious land of Grunia.

'We've got to find out more about those people,' said Toby. 'They're in trouble. What *can* we do, David?'

But David had already decided. He stuffed the transistor set into his pocket.

'We make up our bunks to look as though we were sleeping in them,' he said. 'Then we get our anoraks on and climb out of the window and we go to Gallows Peak. That's what we do. Come on—hurry up!'

The pointer moved from 0 towards 1. Suddenly there
was a quavering, almost faint hissing sound.

CHAPTER 2

THE MONSTER STRIKES

WHILE David carefully arranged their bunk-beds to look
as if someone was sleeping in them, Toby dutifully got
out the anoraks. Then he raised the window a little way
and peered out.

He knew exactly how to lower himself over the window
sill, get a firm grip on the gnarled branches of the old
wistaria, and climb safely to the ground, for this would
not be the first time the two boys had slipped out on
some night adventure.

The moon was high and the sky was cloudless: there
would be light enough to see the path even in the depths
of Troll Wood, through which they had to pass. But
Toby wasn't happy. He likes his comfort and, judging
from the biting air that swept into the room, the journey
was going to be most uncomfortable.

'Why should we have to go to Gallows Peak?' he
grumbled. 'It's freezing outside.'

'Well, put your anorak on then,' said David unsym-
pathetically. 'I'll tell you why we're going to Gallows
Peak. Our village is in a hollow of the hills and I think
they may interfere with radio reception. If we climb up
higher we may get clearer and louder signals on the
transistor set. And that's what we *want* to get, isn't it?'

'Oh, I suppose so. Let's be moving, then.' And Toby
slid over the sill and clambered down to the ground.
David switched off the light in the bedroom and followed him, carefully lowering the window as he left.

They slipped across the road, over the stile into the
fields, and, with elbows held close to their sides, jogged
down the path into the valley, through the end of Troll
Wood, and on to the slope of White Star Hill.

There they slowed down for the long haul past the big
White Star, cut into the chalk of the hillside, and up to
the cairn of stones that marked the top of Gallows Peak.

They were within a few hundred feet of the crest when,

11

suddenly, dark clouds began to sweep across the sky and, turning to look back, they saw waves of white mist rolling up from the valley below, rising and spreading until Troll Wood vanished under the white blanket, then their own village of Dingle Down, then the slopes of the hill immediately below them. And still the white tide kept on rising.

'Quick!' urged David. 'There's Gallows Peak Farm—let's get inside before the mist blots out everything.'

The old ruin still had four stout walls and a sturdy roof of stone, but its door and windows had long since vanished.

'Might as well get as high as we can,' advised David, leading the way up a worn stone staircase to the upper rooms. 'Now let's try the transistor set again.'

Now that the effort of climbing was over, however, the two boys had begun to feel the bitter cold. Toby leaned back against the window-ledge blowing into his cupped hands and then pushing them under his armpits.

David switched on the set and began to turn the pointer but he was shivering so much that it kept jerking from one side of the dial to the other.

'You'll never get anything while you're holding it in both hands,' said Toby irritably. 'Put in down on the floor.'

So David did so, lying flat on the rough planks himself and holding the set down with one hand while he did his best to turn the pointer smoothly with the other.

At last the loud-speaker responded with the familiar hissing sound. This time there was no crackling. The hissing grew to a dull roar.

'That's better,' said Toby, now full of interest.

'I thought it would be. Quiet! We're getting somewhere now . . .'

The roaring noise faded rapidly to a deep, velvety silence. A second later there was a sharp click and—so clearly and close that it might have come from a person in the same room—a deep voice said: '*Here speaks Brindor, Tidings-Bearer to the Folk of Grunia. Take warning! Hildrok the Outcast has returned. He has let loose the Wurgs upon our land. Until further tidings as to our defence can be given, keep to your homes by night, and by day enter not the forests and dark places save in numbers.*'

12

The voice was suddenly drowned by the roaring noise again.

'You've lost him! Can't you get him back?' cried Toby.

'I'm trying . . . I'm trying . . .' David snapped. He pressed his ear close to the loud-speaker and fiddled with the dial while Toby watched him anxiously.

So it was that neither of the boys saw a long, black, rubbery kind of rod slide, snake-like and soundless, over the window-ledge from the darkness outside.

It paused, quivered a moment, then the probing tip of the thing touched Toby's jeans.

At once, in a lightning-swift movement, it wrapped itself twice round his body and closed tightly over his mouth as he opened it to cry out.

'I thought I'd got him again, but I haven't. You come and try, Toby,' said David, looking up from the floor.

But Toby wasn't there.

'*Toby*! Come here and help me!'

David stood up. White cloud covered the window-opening, curling long woolly fingers into the room. Now and then the swirling mist would light up with a pale glow as the moon was for a few moments uncovered.

'*Toby*! Why on earth do you go wandering off at a time like this!'

No answer.

David got up angrily, switched off the transistor set and stuffed it in his pocket.

'Don't lark about, you idiot,' he called and tramped into the other room. No-one there.

David peered down the stone steps.

'*Toby . . . TOBY*!'

Silence.

Suddenly David had an idea. On the other side of the room there was a big clothes cupboard built into the wall beside the old fireplace.

It would be just like Toby to be hiding in there, giggling to himself while his brother searched for him.

David tiptoed across the room, turned the knob and flung open the heavy door. The cupboard was empty.

Angry, but now very much alarmed, David turned. And suddenly he froze.

From the white mist outside, something, like a thick,

13

heavy rope, came snaking over the window-ledge into the room and began to wave about as if it were seeking something.

Behind it, slowly rose two glowing spots of red light that rolled from side to side and grew ever larger.

EYES!

David gasped. The eyes swung towards him. A low, hideous snarling sound came from the window. In sheer terror David leaped for the shelter of the clothes cupboard and slammed the heavy door shut, gripping the steel catch on the inside of the door and pressing it into place with all his strength. As he did so something struck the door with a thud that shook it from top to bottom. Again and again the thing outside battered at David's refuge.

He cowered back into the depths of the cupboard, trying desperately to fight down panic. If the creature could not open the door it seemed determined to break it down. David's mind raced. What could he do to help himself? And then, in the pause while the monster seemed to be bracing itself for an even mightier blow, the answer came to him.

This is what he did: with the tip of the little finger of his left hand he touched the base of the first finger of his right hand and said into the darkness: 'This is David Green calling Captain Septimus Cobwebb! Please help, Uncle Septimus! Toby's vanished and I'm being attacked . . .'

His voice was drowned by a resounding crash that split the stout wooden panel in front of him. Through the crack a red beam from the eye of his attacker shone full on David's face. There was a long, chuckling snarl of triumph, then silence. David felt certain that the monster was drawing back and gathering all its forces for the final assault.

There may be some of you who haven't yet met the mysterious uncle—Captain Septimus Cobwebb—to whom David had just called for help. If there are, I'll tell you all about him later, because now, with David trapped in this dark cupboard and death at the very door, there really isn't time.

A sudden slithering sound told David that the beast was on the move and he braced himself for the crash of its body against the door.

14

But the crash did not come. Instead the slithering sound grew nearer. Something was sliding over the surface of the door. Through the crack the great red eye again sent a shaft of baleful light. Close beside the crack a strange buzzing began and suddenly a circle of wood, as perfectly shaped as if it had been drilled out, fell at David's feet. And through the hole that remained there came the rope-like thing—the antenna, the tentacle, whatever it was—glowing red in the light from the creature's eyes.

This time, however, there was no indecision about its movements. It did not wave, questingly, from side to side. With wicked, stabbing motions, it stretched forward, closer and ever closer, to strike down its prey.

This was the end. There could be no escape now. David flung himself flat against the back of the cupboard and braced himself for the fatal blow.

As he did so, the silence was suddenly broken by a burst of crazy chuckling. Then, close to his ear, a queer, metallic voice said: 'Come on, David Green. Don't dilly-dally! Your Uncle Septimus wants to see you.'

And with that it seemed as if the bottom fell out of the cupboard and David found himself plummeting like a stone through the darkness below.

CHAPTER 3

A WILD RIDE IN THE NIGHT

WELL, now, while David and Toby are going—or rather being taken—to wherever-it-may-be, I'll tell you as quickly as possible about the mysterious Uncle Septimus Cobwebb. Long ago, when this uncle was a boy himself, he'd gone at night into a meadow where there were some of those green circles in the grass that people call fairy-rings. He left a note to his father saying that he was going to sit in the centre of one of those rings until the fairies appeared. Uncle Septimus never came home again but one day he sent a message telling the Cobwebb family and their relations a way of getting in touch with him if they needed his help. If David and Toby were ever bored,

15

for instance, and wanted an adventure they had only to call Uncle Septimus and, *whoosssh*, an adventure started right away.

All the boys had to do to get in touch with Captain Cobwebb, as he was known in the strange country where he lived, was to press a little blue spot that he had put at the bottom of the first finger of their right hands (remember how David did it?), then speak their message. But if it's as easy as that, why hadn't Toby called for Captain Cobwebb's help?

The answer is that he couldn't. His arms were tightly pinned to his sides and even if he could have brought his hands together it would have been no use because he was unable to open his mouth to speak.

So, with his eyes fixed despairingly on his brother, who was bending anxiously over the transistor radio set, Toby found himself swept from the room into the cold, clammy darkness outside. Slowly, slowly, he was being carried downwards.

If only he could have managed to warn David, Toby thought. David would have known what to do. At least, if he had been unable to help, he would have known what had happened to his brother. But now . . . as soon as David looked up and saw Toby was no longer there, his first thought would be to search the house for him. He would think Toby was playing a trick on him and it could be *ages*, Toby thought miserably, before David came to the conclusion that something was really wrong. When he did though, he'd be sure to call for help from Uncle Septimus. That idea made Toby feel a bit more hopeful.

He was still being carried down, very slowly, towards the ground. Toby twisted himself around a little and tried to look along the tentacle that gripped him so firmly. It vanished into the mist, but, straining his eyes, he glimpsed from time to time two glowing red dots. As he was carried down, these also moved down at the same rate. They must be the eyes of the creature that was holding him.

And then Toby saw something more. A few feet away two other eyes came into view through the mist. And these eyes were moving upwards . . . towards the rooms above and the unsuspecting David.

Clearly, the monsters were highly intelligent creatures,

16

or they were directed by some intelligent power, for their plans had been cleverly laid. Very soon now David would be captured, pinioned and gagged like Toby had been, before he could get a message to Uncle Septimus. And then what would happen?

There seemed to Toby to be now only one very faint glimmer of hope: the monsters had set out to capture both him and David and, whatever they meant to do to them in the end, it was pretty certain that they would first take the two boys to their headquarters. If the boys were left together for even a short time, they could work out a plan of escape. Toby was sure of that.

The monster seemed to have reached the ground now. The tentacle gripped harder, drew him closer, and Toby found himself held firmly, face down, on something that felt like a hard, slightly-curved plate of metal covered with a thick coating of hard grit, like very coarse sandpaper. He was glad, as they picked up speed, that his hands were not rubbing against it and that his jeans protected his knees, for the friction, as the monster undulated across the tussocks of grass, would soon have ripped the flesh from his bones.

He tried to make a picture in his mind of what the monster was like. As he was doing this, right below his face there appeared two thin slits of red light, side by side. The slits widened, the light grew stronger and Toby found himself being regarded by two big, red, bulbous, staring eyes. These looked at him fixedly for about ten seconds—and ten seconds is quite a long time when a monster's eyes are only a few inches away from your nose—and then they slowly closed.

In that time Toby had put several facts together and got a clear idea of what the creature must look like. It was large, flattish, dish-shaped. It travelled close to the ground, without any of the bumpy motion he would feel if it had legs. Its skin—or shell—was very rough. And its eyes—and here was the vital clue—were on top of that flattish body.

'It's something like a flat-fish,' Toby told himself,— 'like a plaice, or a sole, or a skate. Only it sort of swims on land, and how it manages to do that I just don't know.'

The motion was not unpleasant, and the grip of the creature's tentacle was so firm, that Toby felt quite secure

17

and lost all fear of falling off. His eyes closed in the darkness and he dozed.

How long this lasted he never knew, but suddenly he was wide awake. There was a jolt as the monster beneath him put on a terrific surge of speed. For a moment a blaze of light enveloped them and Toby *saw* . . .

They were just above the surface of a road. Ahead lay an open gate into a field. The lights that blazed upon them were the headlights of a car, roaring down on them out of the mist. Toby had one glimpse of the creature that was bearing him—gigantic, shield-shaped, the edges of the shield fringed with thousands of white filaments that undulated from end to end of the creature so rapidly that it seemed to be surrounded by foaming surf. The car horn blared. The headlamps seemed about to engulf them. The monster was clearly terrified. One tentacle contracted around Toby, almost squeezing the breath from his lungs. The other waved frantically about, trying to shield the tender eyes of this creature of the night from the blinding beams.

All this Toby saw in a fraction of a second. Then the darkness closed around them. From behind there came the frantic squeal of brakes applied in panic, then the crash of metal on stone, the shattering of glass. Then silence. Below Toby the body of the monster throbbed with the wild energy of terror as it fled from the lights that had stabbed its delicate eyes with searing pain.

Toby had been frightened, too, and like a lot of us, as soon as the immediate danger had passed he felt the need to blame somebody. The motorist wasn't there— he was in fact cowering in his wrecked car, too frightened by what he had seen to crawl out of it. So it was the poor monster that had to bear Toby's displeasure.

'You fatheaded flat-fish!' he muttered. 'Why don't you look where you're swimming—or whatever you think you're doing? You might have killed me!' Of course when you're as angry as Toby was you really feel better if you shout. But that black, rubbery tentacle was still clapped firmly over his mouth. So he registered his protest in the only way left to him: he raised one leg and brought his foot down with a hearty thump on the monster's back.

He shouldn't have done it.

Almost immediately he heard a whistling sound and,

The sight of a boy riding a giant fish is enough to drive anyone round the bend. Farmer Jenkins, however, drove himself straight into a ditch.

with a crack like a revolver, the monster's free tentacle landed a stinging blow on his behind.

'Ouch!' grunted Toby.

'*Crack*!' went the whiplash again . . . '*Crack* . . . *crack* . . . *crack*!'

Toby gritted his teeth, determined not to make another sound, and took his punishment like a man.

Just below his nose one large red, very bloodshot eye opened slowly, glared at him, and slowly closed. Toby took the hint and decided not to get tough with the monster again.

He found it far too humiliating to be flogged by a fish.

CHAPTER 4

THE COUNCIL OF CREATURES

As for David, there were a good many things he wanted to say to his rescuer but the speed of his fall through the darkness took his breath away. At last, just as he felt he could bear the pain in his chest no longer, the crackly voice said 'Air brakes on!'

Something caught at the shoulders of his jacket. There was a great jerk and it seemed for one terrible moment as if his arms would be torn from their sockets. But all was well. Swiftly the speed of his fall slowed and he floated gently and easily downwards. David filled his lungs in one long, sobbing breath. His feet touched gently on solid ground, the pull on his jacket was released and he stumbled forward, gasping. Something light touched his shoulder. Something soft brushed his cheek and the strange voice chuckled in his ear. 'Not so bad, was it, after all? See that spot of light ahead? We're nearly there. Hurry up! Captain Cobwebb will be waiting.'

'Thank you, thank you for bringing me!' said David and he strode ahead. The passage was dark and long, but at last he came out, blinking, into the dawn light through the heavy arched roots of a great tree, festooned with rampant ivy, that hid the entrance to the underground way.

A strange and wonderful sight was before him.

He was standing at the bottom of a huge bowl cut out of the earth. There were ledges all round it that rose in tiers right to the high rim, around which stood closely the dark columns of enormous trees.

At the far side of the arena, set back among the terraces, was a large slab of white marble and in it a door of bronze which now began to open.

In the centre of the arena, right in front of David, stood a large oak table. A chair stood on his side of the table, and on the other side was a much larger chair with a very high back. As David looked, astounded, the big chair was suddenly moved, as by an unseen hand. David saw on the red-leather back the letters C.C. in black, set against a golden cobweb.

'It's Uncle Septimus!' gasped David.

'Then don't dawdle!' said the squawky voice of his rescuer. 'Come and meet him.' And turning his head towards the voice, David saw the speaker. It was a big grey parrot. The bird gave one quick glance at David's stare of amazement then, with a long throaty chuckle, it fluttered across to the table and perched on the high back of the big chair.

'Mission completed, Captain,' said the parrot.

'And speedily accomplished,' answered a deep voice from the empty chair. The parrot ducked its head and wiggled its shoulders with pleasure and David just *knew* that it was being tickled.

'Welcome to our Council, David,' the deep voice said. 'Come forward and take your seat.'

As David walked eagerly towards the oak table he saw that the benches around the huge arena were rapidly filling with animals of all kinds. They were pouring out from the open door behind Captain Cobwebb's chair and going off to left and right to their places. There were owls and hawks, and crows and magpies (who all flew to their perches in the highest rows), corncrakes and pheasants and ducks and geese and hens (who took lower places) and then a whole cloud of smaller birds—thrushes, tits, robins and sparrows and even a few wrens. These all clustered together in an excited, twittering mass. Below them were the four-legged animals—alert, inquisitive foxes; a badger or so, deep in thought; a hare, and a scurry of hopping rabbits. Finally, as David neared the table, the larger visitors arrived—a few sheep, a black sow with half a dozen squealing piglets, a placid cow, an elderly and distinguished old cart-horse and—last of all—an enormous black bull, as big as a removal van.

The bull took one look to see that no other animal was behind him, then he leaned his vast bulk against the big bronze door and slammed it shut. Turning his broad back to the door he sat down, planted his forelegs wide apart, blew two long jets of steam from his nostrils and gave a grunt that shook the earth.

At once the chattering, twittering, squealing, squeaking, cawing, baa-ing, yapping and moo-ing stopped and there was complete silence. David reached his chair and held out his hand politely across the table. It was seized in a strong grip and warmly shaken. 'Be patient a little longer, David,' urged the voice of Captain Cobwebb. 'When I have spoken I want every animal to hear what you have to tell us, for I think you may hold the secret of the strange rumours that have put fear into their hearts.'

'But Uncle,' said David anxiously, 'how will they know what I'm saying?'

'Speak to them as you speak to me,' answered Captain Cobwebb. 'Among us there are no barriers to understanding. Let us begin.'

The big chair suddenly slid backwards as though its occupant had moved it in order to stand up, and the voice of Captain Cobwebb rang out:

'Members of the Council of Creatures! In recent days a number of you have come to me, saying that there is the scent of blood in the air and the wind brings whispers of terror. We all accept the law of existence that some animals must die to feed other animals. But now, in nest, in den and in burrow, the murmurs go that there is some new creature at large that does not kill for food but for the evil joy of killing. From this creature, so it is said, no other animal is safe.'

A wave of low growls, chirping and chattering ran round the arena until it was silenced by a warning rumble from the big black bull.

'Before we talk of action,' went on Captain Cobwebb, 'we must know how far these rumours are true. Already I have sent out scouts, farther beyond the borders of this land than ever before, to seek the facts.

'Only a few minutes ago there came a call for help

22

from my nephew who lives far from here, saying that he was being attacked. I arranged his rescue and sent Parrot to bring him to me. Parrot glimpsed the attacker through a door that it was breaking down to get at the boy. He says it seemed to be a snarling beast of great bulk. It had eyes that glowed like the Red Planet in the sky, and long, searching tentacles. Now let us hear what David can tell us.'

David stood up and took a deep breath. Then, very clearly and as briefly as he could, he told the Council of Creatures every detail of what had happened that night up to the moment of his rescue.

When he spoke of the mysterious warning over the air there was a great stir among his listeners. At the name of Hildrok Captain Cobwebb uttered a long 'Aaahh!' A shudder ran round the arena and the creatures began to work their way quickly down towards the ground until they were crammed together in a mass surrounding the big table.

As David reached the end of his report the parrot said suddenly: 'First scout reporting, Captain!'

A spot of white appeared against the dark circle of trees that rimmed the arena and, as silently as thistle-down, a big white owl drifted down and came to rest on the table.

'You are soon back,' said Captain Cobwebb. 'Have you anything to report?'

For a moment the owl did not reply. It fixed its big round eyes on David and walked up and down inspecting him minutely.

'Oh, come along, old hooter,' snapped the parrot impatiently. 'That's only a boy. Have you never seen a boy before?'

The owl turned round.

'That's just it,' it said. 'I have. Barely ten minutes' flight from here, within sight of the borders of Grunia. I saw a monster with huge eyes that shone red. It floated over the fields like a fish swims in water. And on its back was clamped a boy—exactly like this one.'

'Then that must be Toby, my brother!' exclaimed David. 'I must go to his rescue. Right away, Uncle Septimus!'

'You shall,' answered Captain Cobwebb. 'But first, tell me, Owl: where do you think this monster was going?'

'It was making directly for the land of Grunia,'

answered the owl. 'By now it will have crossed the border.'

'You hear that, David? Once over the border your mission will become even more perilous because I can give you no magical aid. The Unseen People, to whom I belong, have agreed never to intervene magically in the affairs of other countries in our world.'

'I'll go, all the same,' declared David stoutly, 'if the owl will show me the direction.'

'Of course I will,' said the owl. 'But you'll need more help than that. Through our President, Captain Cobwebb, I put the question to the Council of Creatures: how can this rescue be carried out and who will help in it?'

For a few minutes there was pandemonium, with every animal talking at once. But gradually the clamour died down at at last, after a short silence, the horse gave a cough. 'I have recruited a small company to attempt a rescue,' he said, 'and we have worked out a plan. The sun is rising and Owl doesn't see too well in the light. But if he will put us on our way then Hawk can take over as spotter. He will be useful in the attack, too. I will carry the boy, since he moves too slowly ever to catch up with the monster. I am no race-horse but I am built for heavy going. I will also carry our assault troops— the three Otter brothers. That makes only six of us, with the boy, but we've talked it over between ourselves and we think that number is sufficient. We're ready to go at once.'

Captain Cobwebb asked: 'Does anyone disagree with the proposal? No-one? Then it is carried. David,' he added quietly, 'the animals have powerful weapons in beak and tooth and claw. I must provide for you, too.' David felt something suddenly tighten around his waist and glanced down to see that he was now wearing a broad belt of supple leather from which an ivory-handled hunting knife hung in its sheath.

David thanked his uncle as the unseen hands of Captain Cobwebb helped him to his seat on the horse's back. The three otters, squealing with excitement as if they were going on a picnic, took their places. One lay at look-out between the cart-horse's ears, the other two took station on David's shoulders, sitting on their hind legs and keeping their balance by hanging on to his hair with one paw while they waved to their friends with the other.

Minutes later the rescue party were looking out across

meadows, woodland, hills and valleys lit by the rays of the rising sun, while the owl pointed out the direction to the hawk and the horse snuffed the air and pawed the earth with one powerful forefoot.

One of the otters on David's shoulder leaned forward to stare cheekily into his face.

'You're puzzled, mate, arntcha?' it said.

'He's wondering why little otters go chasing big monsters,' giggled Number Two. 'Arntcha, boy?'

David admitted that he was.

Number Three, lying between the horse's ears, turned his head.

'Owl says this monster's a sort of fish,' he said. 'See?'

'We got a kind of interest in fish,' said the giggler, Number Two.

'And the bigger the fish . . .' said Number One.

'. . . the bigger the dish,' spluttered Number Two.

'So don't worry about your brother, boy,' said Number Three, 'because this monster fish is going to be the one that *didn't* get away. See?'

And with that the hawk cried out, the three otters screeched 'Gee up! Gee up!' the great horse lurched forward, and the strangely assorted band of warriors was on its way to track down the mysterious monster and rescue Toby.

CHAPTER 5

THE BATTLE OF THE CAVERN

Toby was feeling very much in need of rescue. He was weary, but too uncomfortable to sleep. He still felt the sting of the spanking that the monster had given him. He was hungry and what was worse than just plain hunger was knowing that he had a pocketful of liquorice allsorts and couldn't move a hand to get them out. It made him furious.

The monster surged along, a little slower perhaps than before, but it showed no inclination to pause. Toby noticed that the mist was becoming thinner and lighter and from time to time he saw formless dark patches which, he thought, might be trees.

Slowly the dawn came. A faint pink glow grew in the sky. Toby saw that the ground sloped steepily upwards. The monster seemed to be worried by the growing light. Instead of keeping to the open meadow land it now sought the shadow of hedgerows and the concealing banks of deep watercourses. Suddenly, it seemed, all the feathered creatures were awake and the warning shouts of blackbirds sent clouds of them whirring into the air as the monster swept beneath the branches where they nested.

The sun came up and a sudden flash of golden light pierced the trees and touched for a moment the monster's head. It leaped as if stung, swung blindly from side to side, missed a projecting rock in the bank of a stream by a hair's breadth, then recovered, sinking lower among the shadows to avoid the light. Toby remembered how the car headlamps had unnerved it. Clearly its eyes were those of a night marauder: in the bright light of day it seemed to be half blinded and in pain.

And now, at last, the monster began to show signs that its mighty strength was ebbing. The way was much steeper than before. Far ahead Toby saw a vast wall of rock. It appeared smooth, towering, unscaleable, yet it was towards that barrier that the monster was urging itself desperately. The trees began to thin out. The meadow grass gave way to a steep scree of grey shale. Streams broke up into fans of trickling tiny tributaries. Still they climbed.

The sky was now blue and cloudless. High, high above, Toby saw a small speck hanging motionless, and wished he could be up there with that hovering bird.

Suddenly, as the monster flung itself violently to one side to seek a patch of shade, Toby heard a new sound. It was a strange sort of humming. The monster seemed to become aware of it at the same time and it suddenly swung to the left. The hum changed rapidly to a clear musical note, then the humming sound took over again. The monster immediately turned slowly to the right, to find the musical note again, and kept to the course it indicated.

'We're being guided in, like an aeroplane!' Toby told himself. 'That means we must be very close to the place

I'm being taken to. But where can it be?' And then he gasped in astonishment. For suddenly, as they turned around the side of a mighty boulder, the goal was in sight.

Straight ahead, a matter of only a few hundred yards, was an enormous square opening at the foot of the cliff face. It looked like the entrance to a railway tunnel, but the sun, shining right into it, showed that its depth was only fifty feet or so. It was just as if some giant had cut a huge cube of rock out of the cliff and carried it off to leave behind this unnatural, smooth-walled chamber.

At the sight the monster seemed to recover its strength. It lunged forward.

As it did so there came from close at hand a loud cry: 'Hold on, Toby! I'm coming!' And as Toby turned his head, a great cart-horse, with David on its back and three strange black figures screeching 'Stand and deliver!' plunged from ambush among the rocks and thundered down upon the monster.

Desperately Toby's captor strove to reach the chamber in the cliff face. The big horse flung itself back on its haunches and came to a stop in a shower of stones. The three black figures—and now Toby saw that they were otters—leaped in front of the monster and began to attack it, each in turn daring death from the whip-like tentacle while the others darted in to sink their sharp teeth and claws into its flesh.

David meanwhile had run ahead to block its path and, pulling his big hunting knife from its sheath, he caught the fierce rays of the sun on the polished blade and flashed them blindingly into the monster's eyes.

But the creature fought back with the strength of desperation. Time and again, with that one free tentacle, it seized one otter after the other and flung them, squealing with rage and frustration, among the rocks.

A spine-chilling shriek from the sky heralded a sudden change in the attack and the otters now closed in from behind the monster while the hawk, who had guided the rescuers to their quarry, swooped down upon the body of Toby, ripping his bonds with its powerful beak and tearing at them with talons of steel.

With the fear of death in its heart the monster now made one last effort to reach the cavern. With a mighty quiver of its heavy body it flung off the three otters and charged headlong at David, who stood barring its way, hurling him to the ground.

Nothing mattered to it now except to save its own life. It passed under the arch of the cavern and, at that moment, the hawk flew into the air with a screech of triumph, the tentacle that had held Toby prisoner for so long fell limp at the fleeing monster's side and Toby rolled to the ground.

David, on his feet again, was dashing to help him, shouting 'It's all right, Toby, I'm coming!' As he reached the entrance he saw, right at the end of the cavern, a long black slit in the rock. He heard a great moan of pain as the monster struggled through it and vanished. But would others come out from there to avenge it?

The cart-horse was ploughing its way up the steep slope to reach the two boys. The crazy otters were dancing up and down squealing 'We've done it, we've done it! We've won! Down with the fishes! Up with the otters!'

David reached his brother, calling 'Are you all right, Toby?' But there was no answer. Toby had fainted. David tried to lift him to his feet. But Toby had laid so long in his bonds that the joints of his arms and legs were locked. It would take hours of patient massage to free them.

There was nothing for it but to seize Toby by the collar and drag him out of the cavern. David started to do so, casting agonised glances back at the place where the monster had disappeared. Progress was painfully slow. Outside, the cart-horse, now nearly at the entrance to the cavern, saw his plight and started towards him.

And just at that moment, with a crash that shook the earth, a ponderous slab of solid rock fell from the roof, like the portcullis of an ancient castle, cutting off David and Toby from their friends, sealing the entrance to the cavern and leaving the two boys to face, in utter darkness, the horrors that lurked beyond the further wall.

*   *   *

David cannot estimate how long he sat beside Toby, trying to massage movement into his limbs, praying for him to recover consciousness, and all the time straining his ears for the sound of menacing movements and his sight for the glow of twin red eyes in the darkness.

But at last Toby stirred. 'Is that you, David?' he asked. 'Where are we? Have we made it?'

'I'm afraid it's bad news,' said David, and he told Toby all that had happened to him, about the rescue team and how, in the very moment of victory, they had been trapped.

'What's more,' he ended, 'it'll be no use calling Uncle Septimus and asking him to get us out. He can't use his magic on this side of the frontier.'

'Well,' commented Toby, 'we're in a pretty bad spot. But we've two things to console us, anyway. First, we're together, so that doubles the chance of escape. Second, at least we've got *something* to eat.'

'Never! Where?'

'In my pocket. Liquorice allsorts. Pull 'em out, David. They may be the last meal—I mean snack—we'll get for some time.'

So they chewed the sweets and began to compare their experiences of the night before. They had been talking for some time when suddenly they found themselves blinking in a shaft of light that shone down on them from high in a wall of the cavern.

A harsh, deep voice grated: 'So! I wanted both of you—and in the end I *have* both of you. Look upon me. Fear, and obey, for no-one can oppose my will and live. I am Hildrok, called the Outcast, but soon to rule all lands I choose beneath the sun!'

With that the light was turned from them to shine upon the speaker.

And David and Toby found themselves gazing up at a being so hideous and repulsive that their hearts turned to ice.

CHAPTER 6

A DISH FROM GRUNIA

THE figure looking down on them had the general outline of a man—a man not less than eight feet tall and broad in proportion, with shoulders that were enormous. But there all human resemblance stopped.

The figure seemed to be hunchbacked, for it stood in

29

a half-crouching position. From the hump there sprang a thick neck, some two feet long, which rose and then curled forward. It joined the head, which was flat and oval resembling that of an enormous snake, at the crown of the skull so that the head hung down, swaying from side to side like the big brass pendulum bob on some mammoth grandfather clock. Long yellow fangs projected from the wide gash of a mouth and a black forked tongue darted in and out between them. From two black slits that slanted, V-shaped, from the sides of the forehead to the centre of the face, unlidded eyes shone with a fierce yellow light. The boys could see neither nose nor ears.

The powerful body was covered with a moss-green growth of short, thick wiry hair except where the neck joined the head, at the wrists and from the knees down. Here the hair gave place to a kind of scaly armour that glimmered with a blue-green iridescence. Hands and feet —or what passed for hands and feet—were long murderous-looking claws, webbed like the hind feet of a giant frog.

This figure, radiating relentless, brutal strength and implacable hate, was Hildrok, called the Outcast. And David and Toby were in his power.

Again the light was in their eyes, blinding them, and from the darkness they heard a horrible scraping from the cavern wall as the steel claws of their captor sought and found a hold on the sheer rock-face.

The two boys huddled closer together. A moment later Hildrok was standing over them.

The harsh voice spoke.

'Do you know why you are here?'

They shook their heads, dumbly.

'I have taken you as hostages. You are of the clan of Captain Cobwebb and close kin to him. If he interferes with my plans you will be killed. Is that clear?'

David said: 'It's clear to *us*. But does Uncle Septimus . . . I mean, Captain Cobwebb . . . know what you propose to do?'

'He will know as soon as he sees that old cart-horse on which one of you came riding this morning. I burned my message into its hide with a branding iron and sent it squealing back to him.'

For a moment Toby entirely forgot his fear. 'That was a filthy thing to do!' he blazed.

30

Hildrok the Outcast. He was part human, part snake and part bird of prey. David and Toby could never agree about all the other parts.

Hildrok roared with laughter.

'It has shown this foolish spell-binder, with his collection of pet animals, that I mean business. That is what matters, not whether the act was good or bad. No, I do not think this uncle of yours will interfere with me.'

'And so long as he doesn't,' said David, 'what are you going to do with us?'

'If he goes on talking, talking, talking, like this. I'll soon be dead of starvation,' muttered Toby bitterly. He'd just been feeling around in his pocket and there wasn't even one little crumb of liquorice allsort left.

'I have no quarrel with either of you,' said Hildrok. He was in high spirits at the thought of how he had got the better of Captain Cobwebb.

Toby, however, was getting in a worse and worse humour. He hated Hildrok, he hated Hildrok's cruelty to the horse and . . . he was hungry. And when Toby is hungry nothing else matters.

So he snapped: 'Well, Mr. Hildrok, if you've no quarrel with us why are you keeping us without food? Do you want us to die?'

'You dare to question *me*!' roared their captor, furious.

'Please, Mr. Hildrok, sir,' said David humbly (while he gave Toby a hefty nudge in the ribs to warn him to shut up), 'my brother doesn't really mean to be rude. He's trying to tell you something that's very important to *you* . . .'

'*Ur-rrr*?' growled Hildrok, his head swung down towards David, the black forked tongue flicking in and out between his yellow fangs.

'You see, it's like this, Mr. Hildrok,' went on David carefully. 'You're certain that Captain Cobwebb won't attack you because he knows you will kill us if he does. But suppose we were to die here, die for lack of food, for instance? We're only small, weak creatures and hunger kills us very quickly. If you were to let that happen, Mr. Hildrok—by accident, of course—then you'd no longer have a hold over our Uncle Septimus Cobwebb, would you?'

Hildrok lifted his frightful head and rested it on one shoulder while he considered this statement. At last he spoke.

'True, true,' he grated. 'I had not thought of it, for I myself eat only once every moon.'

'Twenty-eight whole days without a meal!' gasped Toby, horrified by the thought.

'Ah, but then I eat well!' Hildrok's laughter rumbled round the cavern until the walls shook. 'An ox, a brace of swine, with a barrel or so of the strong wine of Grunia to wash down the food. That was my meal not long ago, on the last quarter of the moon, and after it I slept the night and next day through. I shall not eat nor sleep again until the moon once more is dying. But you—you must feed as often as the sparrows! Tell me, in a day, how many times do you need food?'

'Three,' said David.

'*Four*, you mean,' Toby corrected him firmly.

'We couldn't keep alive on less,' said David, hoping this would satisfy Toby and he would keep his mouth shut.

'Yes, and we need snacks in between meals, too,' (Toby was determined to try his luck as far as it would go). 'We get weak and sick very quickly if we don't have a little something between meals. Because of the energy gap,' he added helpfully.

'No more, no more!' Hildrok seemed almost friendly now. 'Truly you are nothing more than birds without feathers. But since you serve my purpose only so long as you live, you shall have food—as much as you will, and,' he added generously, 'the meat cut from the carcase fresh and warm, as soon as the beast is slaughtered.'

'Ugh!' gurgled Toby, turning as green as Hildrok's hairy hide.

'Alas,' David put in hastily, 'I fear we cannot eat raw meat. It is too strong for our weak stomachs.'

'Weaklings you are indeed!' laughed Hildrok. 'But I will find something to please you. I have a Grunian slave, a mere child like you, who serves my needs. The meat I give him he burns on a fire to suit his weak digestion and he makes strange dishes from roots and leaves. You shall tell him what food you need and he will prepare it according to your orders.'

'Oh, thank you!' said David and Toby together and Toby added: 'Please, will it be a long time before we can eat?'

Hildrok waved a pointing claw and as he did so, the pool of light around them slid suddenly across the floor of the cavern and glowed on the sheer rock face of the

B

opposite wall. High, high, near the roof, a patch of blackness marked the opening from which they had first seen his fearsome face looking down on them.

'No time at all,' answered Hildrok. 'Only as long as it takes you to climb up there.' And he spluttered with laughter at the look of horror on the faces of David and Toby. 'Come!' he said. 'I will show you how to climb. Stand up.'

As they did so, trembling with fright, he hooked a long, curved thumb-claw through the neckband of each boy's jacket and stalked over to the wall, carrying them as if they weighed no more than a feather. To David and Toby the wall looked as smooth as polished marble with no trace of even the tiniest hole or fissure. Yet Hildrok seemed to scratch it with only the very tips of his claws and he went swarming up it as swiftly and effortlessly as a fly running up a window-pane.

He put them down in the opening into the rock and the light that had lit their ascent seemed to be sucked into the passage that lay ahead, making clear their path as Hildrok urged their steps forward.

Soon they turned a corner and found themselves at the entrance to a room. The light seemed to spread itself gently over the walls, filling the place with a gentle amber glow.

The boys looked around in wonder. Clearly Hildrok was not a person who cared for home comforts. A long bench cut in the wall and covered with the skins of deer was all he had to serve for bed or seat, and an oblong block of rock with a flat smooth top, which stood alongside, was apparently intended as a table. In one corner was the entrance to another passage.

Unlike the cavern below, this room was warm and full of a wonderful, appetising fragrance, faint but tantalising . . . teasing Toby's memory with hints of a luscious dish he ought to remember but, as yet, could not.

'Sit. Rest,' commanded Hildrok and as they sank thankfully among the soft skins on the bench he roared: 'BOY! Zillon! Come!'

Almost at once a slim figure glided barefoot and silent from the darkness of the second passage and stood before Hildrok with head bowed submissively. He was a boy, about the height of David (who, as you know, is about two inches taller than Toby), but he was much thinner

34

than either of them. He wore a one-piece garment of coarsely woven undyed cloth, short and sleeveless, with a makeshift belt of rope knotted round his waist. The boy had a snub nose and David caught a questioning glance from blue eyes as he passed them. Not a boy you would pick out of a crowd, had it not been for one thing: his head was covered by a mass of tight, fiery-red curls.

'Zillon,' commanded Hildrok, 'these boys are hostages and need food. Raw meat offends their stomachs. Perhaps the food you eat will be more to their taste. Try them, but if they cannot eat it then you must find something to their liking, for I will not have them go hungry. See to it!'

As Zillon bowed, Hildrok turned to David and Toby.

'Have food, then rest,' he said striding from the room. In the passage he turned, 'Do not think of escape,' he warned. 'There is no way out, either through Zillon's quarters or from this room. I shall be back later in the day.'

A door of rock slid gratingly across the entrance to the passage. Zillon turned to the boys and smiled.

'You look hungry,' he said. 'I was just preparing a meal for myself when you arrived. You shall taste it and if you like it then I shall make as much as you want, quickly.'

'It smells all right,' said Toby cautiously. ''What's in it?'

'We take the flesh of a creature that inhabits the waters of these parts,' answered Zillon, 'and with it the root of a plant, which is divided in a special way. We put them together, heat them strongly amid blue smoke and then anoint them with a sour wine before eating.' He paused and looked at Toby's glum expression. 'My people account it a delicious dish,' he pleaded. 'Please do not condemn before you have tasted.'

David trod heavily on his brother's foot.

'Of course we'd like to try it,' he said. 'And thank you very much.' But Zillon was already on his way.

In a short time he was back, bearing two large pieces of slate on which, as he laid them before the boys, they saw a heap of some yellow substance that gave off a strong aroma.

Toby and David gave one look, took a deep breath,

and suddenly thrust out grasping fingers and began to stuff the material into their mouths!

Zillon looked aghast. 'Oh, forgive me!' he cried. 'I forgot to bring you eating tools. I go . . .'

But Toby halted him with a commanding gesture and paused just long enough in his eating to make a strange pronouncement.

'Yudoneeniefaforforfiyachi.'

Which, being translated, means: *'You don't need knives and forks for fish and chips!'*

CHAPTER 7

THE PIT OF WURGS

IT was only after Zillon had returned from his tenth trip to his kitchen that David and Toby, with great sighs of pleasure, pushed their plates away, praised the blushing Zillon for his wonderful cooking and got down to questioning him about the people of Grunia and Hildrok and why he should want to make war on them.

'My people,' Zillon told them, 'are peaceful folk. For generations they have been farmers and herdsmen, living simply, harming no-one. But always there has lain over us the shadow of an ancient prophecy. This said that deep under the earth there still lived great monsters, millions of years old, and that one day they would find their way into our world and bring destruction upon us. Well, the years passed and they were peaceful. Only the very old folk ever talked of the prophecy and boys like me laughed at them when they did so.

'And then came Hildrok. One day a woodsman on his way to cut timber heard a faint cry coming from a clump of bushes. When he pulled these aside he found a tiny puling creature, unlike any animal he had seen before. It was lying in a fox's abandoned earth and it was clearly starving. He brought it back to the city, where everybody pitied and marvelled at its strangeness and it was coaxed back to life, put in a pen in a farmer's yard and cared for . . . out of curiosity, I think, to see what it would become.

'It grew rapidly and when it learned to speak, some said it must be human, while others shook their heads. The farmer named the creature Hildrok and tried to teach him to be useful about the farm, but without success. He grew rapidly and as he grew so did his temper and his savageness. Time after time cattle were found slain in the fields and soon the deaths were traced to Hildrok. Men tried to bind him but he broke loose. He took to the woods and one night he returned to the farm that had been his home and slew the farmer and his family.

'So the whole city went out with weapons and they caught Hildrok. They brought him to this mountain, where there was a small cave. They flung him in and sealed the entrance with huge rocks—for that is the punishment decreed by law for his crime. All thought that we had done with Hildrok for ever. The years passed peacefully again.

'And now—Hildrok is back and through him the prophecy is being fulfilled! Somehow, in trying to escape, he must have found his way through caverns and watercourses, deeper and deeper in the bowels of the earth until he stumbled on the world of these prehistoric monsters. How he controls them I do not know but it is Hildrok who has brought them into our world and he is using them to avenge himself upon the people of Grunia. They will destroy us and so the ancient prophecy will be fulfilled . . .

> *Grunia shall lie in ruins*
> *And the flesh of its people*
> *Shall be food for the Wurgs.'*

'Wurgs? Why, that's what we heard them talking about on your transistor,' exclaimed Toby excitedly. But David shot him a warning glance. 'No, that was something else,' he said. Until now he'd forgotten all about the transistor set. He felt his pocket. It was still there. He might be able to make some use of it, he thought, but he wasn't ready to say anything about it to Zillon until he was sure he could trust him.

'The Wurgs haven't destroyed Grunia yet, Zillon,' said David. 'Why should this thing *have* to happen?'

'Who can stop it happening?' asked Zillon, sadly. 'The end has already begun. Who can defy the might of

Hildrok? Who can fight against these great beasts, the Wurgs? My people asked of the Wise Woman what chance there was of salvation. But the answer showed us that there was indeed no hope.'

'Why, what did she say exactly?' asked Toby. He liked stories about curses and oracles and wise women and that kind of thing.

Zillon smiled bitterly. 'These were her exact words:

> *"The bars of Fate at last shall crack*
> *When a child rides by on a monster's back."*

'And what chance,' snorted Zillon, 'what chance is there of *that* happening?'

'None at all, I reckon,' David agreed, glumly.

But Toby cried: 'Hey, wait a minute! What about *me*? I don't like people calling me a child, but I suppose I am one. And *I* came riding into Grunia this morning on the back of an enormous old Wurg, didn't I, David?'

The boys told the excited Zillon about the way Toby had been kidnapped by the Wurgs, about Captain Cobwebb and how Hildrok came to be holding them as hostages.

'Then,' cried Zillon, 'you have fulfilled the prediction, Toby. Through you Grunia shall be saved!'

But Toby, who knows hundreds of story-book predictions off by heart, was a bit more cautious.

'Your old Wise Woman said only that the bars of Fate would *crack*,' he warned. 'She didn't say they'd *break*. They won't break by themselves, will they? Somebody's got to *do* something about getting them broken, haven't they?'

'I will do anything to save my country from destruction,' answered Zillon.

'Then we'd better get our heads together,' said David, 'and work out a plan. One of us at least has got to get out of here . . .' David's quick ear caught the sound of a stealthy movement behind them.

'And that reminds me,' he went on, raising his voice so much that Toby and Zillon stared at him in surprise, '. . . we have a dish in our country that we like very much, Zillon. I wonder if you have anything that resembles it? We call it sausage and mash . . .' He broke off.

Hildrok was standing over them.

'I gather from your talk that you have eaten well and are out to test Zillon's skill,' he said. 'However, I do not think it wise to leave you too long together. Zillon, to your quarters!' Hildrok walked behind Zillon as he left the room, then turned. 'I close the door, so,' he said as the slab of rock slid into place. He pointed to Toby. 'You will remain locked in this room. And you . . .' he tapped David on the shoulder, you will come with me. I mean to show you my power—the army which will go on ravaging the land of Grunia until its people plead for mercy. Already the day is dying. At nightfall you shall see us set forth. You will stay sealed in the great cavern until my return. Go!' And pushing David before him into the other corridor, he closed the door behind him. This time the light followed him and Toby was left alone in darkness.

Once more David was picked up by Hildrok and the glow went with them into the great cavern below. Hildrok stalked across to the end wall. In one corner he opened a door and thrust David through. The weird light flickered on a vast domed ceiling of rock and faded away down the walls into the unfathomable darkness. The air was hot and thick with a fetid smell. From the depths rose a chorus of fearful snarls that echoed and re-echoed from the rocks in a terrifying crescendo.

'Watch!' commanded Hildrok.

The light grew and grew until David found he could see right down to the bottom of the great gash in the rock. It was like standing on some Alpine snow-peak and gazing down to the distant floor of the valley below. But here there was no beauty, only horror. As far as the eye could span across, as far as it could see along the valley, the ground was covered with the snarling, snapping, undulating, weaving bodies of creatures like the one that had kidnapped Toby.

'My army,' said Hildrok, '—my invincible army! All hungry and eager for food. See, here is the road up which they come to hunt their prey by night.' He pointed to his right and David saw that from the depths of the valley, up to the slit in the wall that led into the great cavern, there was a long, smooth, wide ramp. It was slippery with moisture and a thin cloud of steam rose from its surface.

'The outer door is opening now,' said Hildrok. 'It is

time to call them.' And with a roar that shook the very walls of rock, he shouted: 'Come, my soldiers! Come my Wurgs! There is food a-plenty for you among the cattle of Grunia!'

Far, far below the snapping and the snarling grew. Then there came a rushing sound as of a great wind. And up the long ramp they came sailing—an enormous, seemingly unending shoal of Wurgs, long black tentacles streaming back, flat against their shield-like shells. They surged like a tide through the slit, into the cavern beyond until David's eyes tired of watching their passage.

At last Hildrok drew him out into the main cavern. Only two Wurgs, larger than any David had seen before, remained within. They rested, side by side, a few inches above the ground, their myriad white filaments gently undulating, long black tentacles standing upright.

In the light that had followed them into the cavern, Hildrok strode across to the waiting Wurgs. Legs wide apart, he planted his mighty claws on the back of each one, seized the tentacles as if they were reins and jerked them smartly. At once his strange steeds shot towards the outside world like shells from a cannon's mouth.

'You will see me again at dawn,' called Hildrok, and in a flash he had vanished into the night. The fortress-door of rock thundered down into place. The light faded away and David was alone in the darkness.

He tried to sleep, and did in fact drop off for a time, but it was a troubled sleep for something was nagging at his mind. At last the message got through and woke him up: that door in the rock, beside the slit that opened on the Pit of Wurgs . . . was there a corridor beyond it? If so, where did it lead? Could he get into it? Perhaps he could discover how Hildrok made the door open and shut. Although he could not see, David felt that his sense of touch might help him find the key to the secret mechanism.

He began to work his way around the walls of the cavern. He came to the corner, turned. Reaching up he felt, at shoulder-height, the slit through which the Wurgs came and went. At length he came to the next corner. It was here that the door was placed. David passed his hands over the rock—up, across, down . . . He pressed every bit of rock that stood out, however slightly. He prodded with his finger or the point of his hunting knife, into every tiny depression, every trace of a fissure. It was no use.

David wondered if he would have any more luck if he could try from the other side of the door? But how to get there, since he couldn't open it? Then the idea suddenly struck him: crawl through the slit that opened on the Pit of Wurgs and work his way along the inner ledge to the place where he had stood with Hildrok. It would be tricky, but . . . He decided to try.

It proved much less difficult than he had supposed. He got through the slit and managed to work himself upright on the ledge inside. With his hands behind his back, touching the wall for guidance, he began to edge himself along.

He managed to progress for about a yard or so, feeling very much relieved at the ease with which he was handling the manoeuvre. All the same, David thought, it would be as well to pause a moment and test the width of the ledge he was on. He put out one foot, gingerly, feeling for the edge. He touched it, ran his shoe from left to right, to check. At that moment his hand slipped on the clammy rock-face behind him. His foot slid off the level ledge on to the curve of the wet, slimy ramp that fell precipitously into the depths below. David fell with a despairing cry. There was a sudden jerk as his jeans caught on something. For a fraction of a second his fall was halted.

Then, with a sharp *rrripp*, the fabric tore and David found himself plunging, with the speed of an avalanche, into the unknown.

CHAPTER 8

ENTER A STRANGE BLACK BUNDLE

As for Toby—well, he was full of good food, he had a couch of warm animal fur to lie on, but he couldn't get on with reading *The Mad Scientist's Revenge* (which he found he had stuffed in a pocket) because there was no light, and he couldn't go exploring Hildrok's domain because he was locked in.

So he very sensibly lay down, rolled himself into a furry cocoon, and slipped into a sound sleep.

41

He awoke suddenly to a chill feeling of danger. A slight noise brought him, fully alert, on to his feet, straining ears and eyes into the darkness. A thin line of yellow light appeared and began, very slowly, to grow wider. And a voice whispered urgently.

'Toby, Toby! Don't be afraid . . .'

'Zillon! It's all right, I'm awake. Come in. How did you open that door, I thought it was locked? And where did you get that light from?'

'One question at a time,' laughed Zillon as he placed his flickering lamp on the table. 'This light? I save the fat from the flesh that Hildrok gives me for my food and I melt it down and put it in this bowl. To make the wicks I pull threads from my garment. Unless I can escape from here,' added Zillon with a wry smile, 'there will come a day when I have to decide whether to have light or to go naked. It is only rarely that Hildrok allows any of that mysterious light of his to remain when he leaves these rooms. As to the door—I watch Hildrok closely as he comes and goes and after many days I have discovered the secret . . .'

'I bet I know it already,' said Toby, who can be a bit of a know-all at times. 'There's a sort of knob in the wall, or something, and you have to press it to work a spring thing that makes the door open or shut.'

'Go find it, then,' grinned Zillon. But though Toby felt the wall all round the doorway and pressed every little lump in the rock that he could find, nothing happened. He cast his mind over all the thrillers and mystery stories he'd read—from *Sir Jasper's Secret* to *Death in the Dungeon*—and he couldn't recall a single case where there wasn't a knob in the wall to be pressed, or pulled. He was baffled.

Zillon came beside him and stroked the wall gently. 'Shut!' he said, and the door closed. 'Open!' It was open once more.

Toby tried—but the door wouldn't work for him.

'I watched Hildrok move his hand like that a thousand times,' Zillon told him, until I realised that the movement meant nothing. It was done simply to fool me. Look at the floor, Toby. See that bit of rock that sticks up? Step lightly on that.'

Toby did so. There was a faint tremor beneath his foot, and the door closed.

'Press to open, press again to close,' said Zillon. 'There is a control on each side of the door.'

Toby was excited. 'But when Hildrok's been out of the way you must have explored every passage there is in this place! Why, you could have escaped long ago!' Toby became suddenly suspicious. 'Why *didn't* you escape, Zillon?' he asked.

'Because there *is* no escape,' retorted Zillon, angrily. 'Through this door is the small cave that is my quarters —and that is all. Through that door is the passage to the great cavern and a wall too smooth to climb down and too high to leap from without smashing every bone in my body. Those are all the passages I know exist. If I *had* found a way out do you suppose I would be here now? What do you think I feel like—unable to help my people, having to serve the creature that is destroying them, and dependent for existence on the food and fuel that he steals from them?'

What could Toby say to that except to apologise?

'Still,' he added, 'there are three of us now, Zillon, not just one. Between us we'll find a way to escape. And we won't be just running away to save our own skins, because once we're out of Hildrok's clutches we'll find a way to beat him and drive him out of your country. Old Scaly-Legs!' said Toby. 'Old Duck-Feet!' Which I don't think he would have said if Hildrok had been there to hear.

Zillon said: 'Why don't we take the light, go to the opening into the big cavern and talk to your brother? He will be feeling lonely, and I am sure that he will have been left in darkness. It will be some hours before Hildrok returns with the Wurgs.'

'Yes, come on,' Toby agreed. 'Let's have a council of war!'

But there was no trace of David in the big cavern and after they had waved the lamp about and called his name until they were hoarse, Zillon said: 'All I can think of is that Hildrok took David with him after all—just to have someone witness his evil deeds and be impressed by his ruthlessness. We shall learn what has happened when the Wurgs come back at dawn.'

Zillon invited Toby to go and look at his quarters. The room, much smaller than the one in which Toby had slept, was even more sparsely furnished. There was just one

43

knee-high rock shelf along one entire wall, and that shelf had to serve Zillon for his stove and cooking pots, for his table and for his bed.

He set the lamp down on the shelf and waved an arm.

'My castle!' he said grimly, '—my castle, Toby, and my prison!'

Toby looked around. On the shelf a handful of embers still glowed within a frame of stones, set in a tiny alcove in the rock wall.

'Is this your cooking fire?' he asked.

'Yes.'

'But,' said Toby, 'there's hardly any soot on the wall. How does the smoke get out?'

Zillon laughed shortly. 'Still looking for that imaginary escape passage?' he asked. 'Put your hand into the alcove behind the fire and feel about.'

Toby did so and his fingers encounted a small hole. It was little wider than his clenched fist and it went upward at a steep angle into the rock. He lay on the stone ledge and peered up the narrow chimney, but he could see no gleam of moon or star.

Zillon said: 'In daytime I have seen a faint glimmer of light. It consoles me to have even that small glimpse of the outside world. But there is no escape for us by that route, Toby—not even if we starved ourselves to skin and bones.'

'That's true. But,' Toby said thoughtfully, 'since it does join us to the world outside, perhaps we could use it to help us to escape.'

Zillon was sarcastic. 'What do you mean?' he asked. 'Shall we make up the fire and sit on the flames until we go up in the flue in smoke?'

'I don't mean that we should try to get out through the flue,' said Toby, patiently, 'but we might use it in some way to get a *message* out.'

'How?'

'Well, like this for instance . . .' And Toby took the flickering lamp and moved it slowly to and fro across the opening of the flue. 'Flash a message for help. That's one thing we might try.'

'But we're right at the top of a huge rock and the light will go up into the clouds, if it goes anywhere. Who do you think will see it—seagulls? And if they do, what will it mean to them? Nothing!' Zillon certainly wasn't enthusiastic.

'Well, I still think we can use it in *some* way,' said Toby, huffily. 'And I'll keep *on* thinking till I get a better idea.'

'I feel,' said Zillon, 'that we should separate now. It will soon be dawn. We must be in our own quarters, with both doors locked, when Hildrok returns. He must not suspect anything.'

So they parted and Toby was innocently dozing when some time later Hildrok strode in, lighting up the room, and pulled him roughly from his couch.

'Take this in your hand,' he ordered. 'Look at it. Feel it. And tell me what you think it is and whence it comes.'

Toby rubbed his eyes and stared. 'It's a piece of blue cloth,' he said. 'And it looks as if it's been torn from my brother's jeans. I mean,' he added in response to Hildrok's puzzled stare, 'I mean it looks as if it's been torn from the clothing he wears upon his legs.'

'I will tell you where I found it,' declared Hildrok. 'It was just inside the opening through which the Wurgs return to their pit. That pit is as deep as the mountains are high and one thing is now sure beyond all doubt— your brother is at the bottom of it, and he is dead.'

Toby was stunned. He tried to speak, but no words came.

Hildrok called Zillon. 'Take the boy into your quarters and keep him there. Never take your eyes from him. I do not intend to lose another hostage. You answer for his life with your own.'

Zillon helped Toby into his own room and they heard the door behind them close.

'I can't believe it!' Toby whispered at last. 'David can't be dead. It's some trick of Hildrok's. He's trying to deceive me for some reason. Don't you think so, Zillon?'

Zillon feared it was all too certain that Hildrok had spoken the truth, but rather than add to Toby's anguish he agreed. 'It may well be so, Toby,' he said. 'No man knows when Hildrok speaks the truth and when he lies. Let us wait, watch and hope. For the present,' said Zillon, 'I will make you an infusion of herbs that will soothe your mind . . .' and he leaned across the rock bench and began to blow on the embers of the fire.

And at that moment a number of things happened at once.

There was a rumbling sound from the chimney flue behind the fire. A great cloud of soot belched from it into the room, covering Zillon's face and neck. As he staggered back, a filthy black bundle shot out from the chimney on to the bench, rolled over several times, checked itself, thrust out two large claws, and hauled itself upright, swaying a little.

Zillon and Toby stood frozen, staring in fearful fascination.

Two large yellow discs slowly appeared at the top of the bundle, rotated like the lamp on the top of a police car, fixed on the two boys and stopped, staring unblinkingly at them.

Slowly two big black wings unfolded. A brisk tremor ran through the beast's body. A cloud of soot rose into the air and was fanned away by the wings.

And there stood, regarding them critically, a large white (well, fairly white) owl. After a moment or two it strolled towards the two boys with a sort of rolling motion, like a sailor ashore, and pushed its beak almost into Toby's nose.

'Yes. There's no doubt about it,' said the owl. 'No doubt at all. You're so much like him that you *must* be his brother Toby. I told Captain Cobwebb that I'd find you before Hawk did!'

CHAPTER 9

IN THE VALLEY OF TERROR

PARALYSED by fear, David hurtled down the slimy ramp at almost jet-speed, twisting and turning, sometimes on his back, sometimes on his stomach, head first, feet first . . . with only one thought in his mind: *what will it feel like when I hit the ground*? But no sensation can last for ever, not even the sensation of fear, and after he had been falling for about ten minutes, without anything happening to him whatever, he began to be able to give some attention to what was going on around him.

This is the Owl as he looked when he emerged at the bottom of Zillon's chimney. He was covered in soot, but he didn't give a hoot as he flew from the flue.

For one thing, with every minute that passed the air was getting hotter and hotter and steamier and steamier until he said to himself: 'If this is anything like a sauna bath then I'm never going to have one.' Then there was a sound of dripping water, which got louder and louder as he fell. It grew to a shrill hissing and to a sound like a cloud-burst. He supposed the 'rain' came from condensation on the cold rocky walls of the vast subterranean valley and from the enormous dome of the roof, incredibly far above.

By now it seemed to him that the ramp was becoming less steep and that his speed was decreasing slightly—though he was still going so fast that, if he were to run into a rock, his skull would be smashed like an eggshell.

Just then he found that the ramp was no longer beneath him! He was falling through space, his body curving in a great arc. And then . . .

With a mighty splash that sent wild echoes flying up and down the length of the rocky valley, David plunged into an invisible lake and the impetus of his fall carried him down, down, down until he felt his lungs would burst. He struggled madly to counter his descent and at last found himself beginning to rise. He paddled furiously to reach the surface and get air, startled as he rose by sudden glimpses of tiny patches of pale light that seemed to be moving around him. But when at long last his head broke water and he found himself swimming they had vanished.

David struck out for the shore, though he had no idea how long he might have to swim to reach it. He began to feel fearful again, for the effort of struggling so far to the surface had left him exhausted. Only one thing made his task easier: the water, he noted with pleased surprise, was warm. In fact, it was very, very warm, and if David had not been so tired and so eager to reach solid ground he felt he would have enjoyed lying on his back and just floating around for hours.

He had not been swimming for long, however, when his feet touched firm ground and soon he was able to crawl from the water on to rock where he lay panting. And now he saw once more the strange lights that he had noticed when he was deep below the water. He saw them as glimmering points of radiance far beneath the surface,

48

circling slowly and now slowly rising. It was as if his plunge into the lake had sent them diving for shelter in the depths and that, now the water was still again, they were returning to the shallows near the surface. As they came nearer he saw that the lights were, in fact, fish—strange, eel-like things, slow-moving and shining with a cold phosphorescence.

David was tempted to slap his hand on the surface of the water and watch them scurry away down until their light faded away in the depths, but he realised that they could be of use to him if he just stayed quiet and watched them.

For now the fish were back in the shallows at the very edge of the water and were spreading out wide apart, each one seemingly taking a stretch of territory and patrolling it slowly. From their positions now David could get an idea of the shape of the lake, for they mapped out a part of its shore like the 'blips' on a radar screen. David saw that the shore-line curved away from him in both directions: he must, therefore, have crossed the lake from the point where the end of the huge ramp overhung it.

There was one small gap in the line of patrolling fish and this, he guessed, might be the point where a stream ran into the lake. But as his eyes grew accustomed to the very faint light shed by the fish, he saw that there was another explanation. First he noted a constant stream of bubbles arising from the depths. Some were very large and burst on the surface with a faint 'plop' after which there came a sudden strong smell, like burning sulphur. After one of these had risen many ripples would spread out from the point where it had burst and the water would appear to boil—as if it were being thrust up in a sudden surge from beneath. 'It's some sort of gigantic spring,' David told himself. 'The water keeps coming up from below, so where I thought there was a stream coming *in* there must be a stream going *out* of the lake. And that's proved by the fish, because when water is flowing into a lake the fish lie with their heads facing the current, to catch any food it brings down. These fish keep away from the spot—obviously there's no food to be had there.

'So,' David argued, 'if I go in the direction that stream is taking at least I shall know that I'm going away from the lake and that I'm going down the valley—because

49

water always flows downhill—and I'll come into the open air again. And then, maybe the hawk will be out patrolling and spot me, or I'll recognise that mountain where Hildrok hides himself and then I'll set about finding a way to rescue Toby and Zillon.'

David felt somewhat rested by now and, thinking these optimistic thoughts about saving himself and then rescuing the others, he got up and made his way carefully to the stream. Then, with his feet in the shallow water and his back to the hot lake, he began to splash his way forward. It was slow going and from time to time, especially if he struck a place where the water seemed to be getting deeper, he would cast about from side to side to check the width and, if necessary, to move towards one bank or the other. Fortunately the stream remained never more than a foot deep at most, despite the ceaseless hissing downpour of water from the towering rock walls of the mighty crevasse that trickled into it through a thousand tiny channels.

David ploughed on for hours and eventually he just had to stop and find a rock on which to sit, draw up his feet and rest his aching ankles. He began to think about the Wurgs and how they had got into the great rock valley in the first place. With the exception of the hot lake, the whole floor of the valley, so far as David could tell, seemed to be of rock and the Wurgs, frighteningly powerful as they might be, weren't built for smashing a way through rock. They must have come up through some break in the surface, somewhere, but where? And suddenly David's mind went back to the hot lake and the streams of bubbles that escaped to its surface through fissures in the rock, far, far below.

'Perhaps that's how the Wurgs got in. *Oh, dear*!' cried David. And with one anguished look over his shoulder he shot off that rock and floundered downstream as fast as he could go.

Hour after nightmarish hour he slipped and staggered along the stream bed. Suddenly, his feet no longer splashed in water. And then the most terrifying thing of all happened. He slipped, put out his hands automatically to try to save himself . . . They hit against solid rock!

The valley had come to an end. It was blocked. David moved from this side to that, testing the rock before him. There was no doubt about it. He could go no further. Nor could he go back now, for even if he found the strength to swim back across the hot lake (supposing no Wurg rose from below to seize him) he could not mount that precipitous, slippery ramp.

And another thought came to him.

By now, in the world outside, the dawn must be near. At any moment Hildrok's huge army of marauding Wurgs would come swooping down in serried ranks to cover the ground on which he stood, snarling, snapping angrily with their rows of massive teeth, and waving those long, searching tentacles, which would surely reveal his presence to them.

He must get to the side of the valley and climb up it as high as he could. David started to mount, steadying himself from time to time against the rock-face that formed the end of the valley.

Far behind him he heard a sudden noise. It grew. He knew well what it was. The Wurgs were returning. Great waves of fetid air swept around him. Already a host of red eyes began to show as distant spots in the blackness.

David was on hands and knees now, scrambling feverishly. The Wurgs flooded the valley. He could see those red eyes—there seemed to be thousands of them—right below him. He put a hand forward, grasping, to pull himself up. The rock crumbled under it. It *wasn't* rock. It was soft shale. Hardly had David realised this than his foot sank through the surface. A moment later it had sunk down to the knee. He heaved and tugged and got it out. And as his foot came free he caught, just for a moment, a glimpse of light. Daylight!

David began to punch away with his feet, trying to widen the hole and as he did so he became aware that the snapping and snarling which had started among the Wurgs had suddenly ceased. He looked down. From a myriad watching red eyes one pair had detached themselves. He saw them growing larger and larger. A Wurg had scented him and in a moment it would be upon him.

He flung himself to the ground. He thrust his arms and head into the hole and strove to dig himself into the ground out of reach of the Wurg's armoury of giant teeth.

David struggled desperately. Earth filled his eyes. The gleam of daylight vanished.

And then keen fangs stabbed his shoulder.

51

CHAPTER 10

LESSON FROM AN OWL

You can imagine how excited Toby was when he heard the owl mention the name of Captain Cobwebb.

'Have you seen David? Is Uncle Septimus going to rescue us? How did you find us, Mr. Owl?' he demanded.

The owl did not answer at once, but its head moved from side to side, very slowly. Then it fixed its big eyes on Toby again and gave him a long stare.

'The correct form of address is not "Mister Owl",' it said. 'I do not address you as "*Mister* Boy". No. "Owl!" will do for me as "Boy" will suffice for you. Correction: as it now appears there are three boys, I shall address you as "Boy Toby", your brother as "Boy David" and this captive here . . . a Grunian, I see, as . . . as . . .'

'As "Boy Zillon", Owl,' said Zillon. 'If you please,' he added politely.

'It is not a matter of whether it pleases me or not,' said the owl severely. 'It is a matter of using the correct terms of address, avoiding, however, unnecessary formality. I see no need for you to call me *tyto alba alba*, for example, although it is my full name. And I am sure you don't wish to be called *Homo sapiens*. A laughable title in any case!' added the owl with a low hoot. 'Ummm. Where were we?'

'The questions, Owl,' prompted Toby.

'Ah, yes. How did I find you? I had been watching a hole for some time. Saw smoke, glow of a fire at bottom of hole at times. A little while back. I suddenly saw a light moving about. Not the light of a fire. More like a candle—anyway, fires do not move about like that. So I came over to investigate more closely. I put my head inside the hole and I heard you talking . . .'

'And that's when you fell down the chimney!'

'That is when I hastened to meet you,' the owl corrected him haughtily. 'On the question of rescue, you know about Hildrok's threat to kill you if Captain Cobwebb interfered with his plans? Well, the Council of Creatures have decided that action must be taken against this evil killer. First, however, you must be rescued. Now we know where you are we can begin to plan. But Hildrok must suspect nothing—for your sakes. What else was it you asked . . . have I seen David? No, I have not. Isn't he here, Boy Toby?'

So then Toby told the owl about David's disappearance and how Hildrok was certain that he had been killed.

'I shall see that Captain Cobwebb is informed about all this,' said the owl. 'But first tell me everything you can about this place under the earth and what goes on inside it . . . when Hildrok comes, when he goes and anything you know about the passageways within the rocks and the doors that guard them.'

It was a long time before Zillon and Toby had finished talking because the owl demanded the most minute details about everything they had observed. At length he was satisfied.

'It is clear to me,' he said, 'that I must stay here and explore this place while Captain Cobwebb directs the search for David and plans are laid to get you both out of here.' The owl rolled purposefully over to the chimney and began to stick his head in.

'You'll get all covered with soot again, Owl!' warned Zillon.

'It's all in a good cause,' answered the owl in muffled tones as he pushed his head further into the flue. 'Now be quiet and do not distract me while I send my message.'

They heard him begin to hoot, calling for a response from any of the other searchers. Within the room the owl's voice did not sound very loud but it was soon clear that he had made contact with some other creature, for he paused a moment then said: 'Very good. Now listen carefully . . .' Every bit of the information that Toby and Zillon had been able to give him was passed on to the unseen listener.

Finally the owl pulled his head from the chimney, fluffed out his neck feathers to shake off a ring of soot and said:

'If you must use that fire, do so for a short time only each day. Remember, any messages that may come to you from our friends outside will have to come down the chimney. I am going to explore Hildrok's fortress from within. In the meantime you must behave as if nothing had happened. Do not offend Hildrok and do as he bids without question. Now show me how these doors are opened and take me to the outer corridor. Every night when Hildrok is away, open the door. If I have anything to tell you I will come to you. It may not be the first night, nor the next. Be patient and do not fear. Now show me the way.'

As they were walking through the big room that Toby called 'Hildrok's study' he ventured—very carefully so as not to offend the owl—to raise a point that had been worrying him.

'You know, Owl,' he said, 'that it's very dark in those corridors. What I mean is, it's not like being out in the forest, you know, where you might get just a glimmer of light from the sky.'

'I appreciate your obvious concern for my safety,' huffed the owl, 'but I'd have you know that owls don't suffer from night-blindness. Why, I have a cousin who can see and catch a field-mouse with no other light than that shed by a candle burning half a mile away. What do you say to that?'

Toby was silenced, but Zillon said: 'Please do not be upset, Owl, but when Hildrok withdraws the light he controls then these corridors are in total darkness. And is it not true that *no eyes* can see in such a case?'

'Oh, dear me, dear me . . .' The owl was clearly exasperated. 'Of *course* it's true. But how little you know about us owls. Stop for a moment. Can either of you produce a small object?'

Toby ferreted about in his trouser pockets but apart from a rather grubby handkerchief and the usual piece of string, all he could produce was a battered brass button with a crown and anchor on it, which he had picked up in the street and kept because he thought it might come in useful. (And, as you will see, it did.)

'That will do,' said the owl. 'Put out your lamp, Boy Zillon. Now, are you satisfied that we are in total darkness? Very well. When I say the word, Boy Toby, throw that button across the room and then hold out your hand, palm upward. Ready? *Now*!'

Toby tossed the button into the darkness. There was a slight chink, but no other sound, and then—barely a second later—the button was dropped into his hand. As Zillon struck flint on steel, coaxing sparks to fire his tinder and then to light the lamp, the owl gloated: 'Well? Are you satisfied? And yet in total darkness no creature can see—as you truly said.'

'But how do you do it, Owl?' asked Toby, amazed.

'By having very good ears,' said the owl, going off into a fit of mixed chuckles and hoots. 'To begin with, owls have larger ears than any other bird. We have wide heads, so our ears are set well apart. When you dropped that button the sound of its fall reached one ear just a fraction of a second before it reached the other and *hup*! I knew at once exactly where the button was.'

'I see!' Toby exclaimed. 'It's rather like a man in a boat taking his bearings. He does it by triangulation,' he said to Zillon, who spread his hands wide and looked blank.

'But *considerably* more quickly,' said the owl hastily.

'I wish *I* could do that!' said Toby enviously.

'I could teach you,' said the owl, as Zillon opened the door for him and he prepared to fly off into the corridor. 'I could teach you, you know, Boy Toby. But there's a snag.'

'What's that?' asked Toby.

'Well,' the owl answered, 'when you took off and you flapped *your* wings, you'd fall flat on your face! *Hoo-hoo-hoo-hoo-hoo-hoo-hoo*! See you later . . .'

And he vanished into the darkness of the outer corridor.

Closing the doors behind them, the boys went back into Zillon's room, Toby making a vow to himself that if ever they escaped from their rock-bound prison he would find and read every book about owls that there was in the world.

Of course, the boys could talk about nothing else but the owl's arrival and the hopeful fact that Captain Cobwebb now knew exactly where they were, while the members of the Council of Creatures were hunting for David.

'We'll get out soon, I'm sure,' Toby told Zillon.

'I have been here so long that I had given up hope,' Zillon answered. 'Now I will try to hope again. Perhaps it will not be . . .' He stopped suddenly as the door slid open and Hildrok strode in.

'Zillon, and you, boy,' he snapped, 'I have brought in two hundred long tree-branches. They are in the next room. Get to work quickly and cut them all to ten feet in length, take off all side-growths. By the time you have finished that task I shall have further duties for you. Smile, Zillon! Smile, for you are preparing for me the weapons that will destroy your city!'

Zillon said nothing but hung his head so that Hildrok should not see the hatred in his eyes.

Hildrok swung on his heel, then paused and cast a keen glance over the table.

'I see you have had a fall of soot,' he commented. 'For the other task I have for you, I shall be bringing some bales of grass. Take a few handfuls, stuff them in the flue and light them. That will burn the soot away.'

Still Hildrok did not go. He ran his finger up and down the table, making patterns in the sooty surface. Suddenly he seized on something and held it up. It was a bird's feather.

'Perhaps this explains the fall of soot,' he said. 'Eh? A bird fell down the chimney?'

'Yes, Master,' faltered Zillon.

'You cannot have cooked it for food, because the fire is out, and besides, I see no bones about. Where is it, then?'

'I cannot say, Master,' quavered Zillon.

Toby broke in to save the situation.

'It was not a big bird,' he said, 'but it brought down great clouds of soot and by the time we had got it out of our eyes the bird had vanished.'

'Vanished? In such a small room? Where could it vanish to, do you think?'

Toby felt that if this went on much longer Zillon might give way.

'It must have gone up the chimney,' he said. 'That is the only solution, for we have searched every nook and cranny, and, as you say, this is a very small room.'

'Of course, of course,' agreed Hildrok, with a smile that Toby did not like at all. 'And it would be easy for it to do that because it was a very small bird. What kind of bird, would you say?'

'Oh, a thrush, or perhaps a blackbird,' said Toby.

Hildrok brushed the soft white feather across his ugly yellow teeth and his grin became even wider.

'Perhaps a blackbird, yes,' he said, 'but it would have to be a white blackbird—an albino blackbird. I have seen one or two about here. And it flew back up the chimney to freedom . . . ?'

Hildrok went to the door but as it opened he turned and looked at Toby and Zillon with a long, cold stare.

'However,' he said, 'there is always a chance that his little white blackbird did not go up the chimney. Perhaps, by some means—which would have to be explained—it got out of this room and is fluttering about, lost in the corridors. I will look for myself. Should it be there it will not escape me. In that case I shall return and seek an explanation—from both of you.' And with that, Hildrok left and the door closed behind him.

Zillon quavered: 'Toby! Our lives are in terrible danger. Don't you see? Hildrok suspects that we know how to open the doors!'

'If he catches Owl he'll be *sure* of it,' muttered Toby. 'And here's the awful thing: Hildrok is stalking Owl *and Owl doesn't know*. And,' he added miserably, 'I just can't think of anything we can do about it.'

CHAPTER 11

A THREAT OF WHISKERS

THE pain in David's shoulder was terrible as the vice-like jaws that held him heaved, pulled and tugged.

Suddenly he felt cold, wet soil close over his legs and feet and he realised that he was not the victim of some Wurg, trying to pull him up out of the earth, but of some other unknown, powerful creature that was pulling him down into it!

Perhaps more than one creature; for now he felt the sleeves of his jacket gripped as well and, amid grunts of effort, he was being dragged forward in the blackness, slowly but surely.

Then, suddenly, it was all over. His body shot forward and downward. The glare of daylight blinded him. And, as soil cascaded from his hair over his face, he landed on a soft slope and began to roll and roll until he was stopped by a low bush and sat up, gasping and blinking.

He was in a grassy clearing on the gentle slope of a wide, wooded sunlit valley, and he was sitting at the foot of a towering wall of rock. As he looked up he could see at the bottom of the rock-face the earth-filled fissure through which he had just been pulled. Three strange black shapes were moving busily around it, packing back earth and piling up rocks to seal the hole.

As he watched, they completed their task, turned, rose on their hind legs and, joining forepaws, they pranced towards David, chanting lustily in praise of their own cleverness:

> We are the Otters, (they sang)
> The brightest beasts that be:
> The rest are simply not as
> Intelligent as we.

> Who are the foremost in the fray?
> Who was it drove the Wurgs away?
> Who was it saved our friend today?—
>   *The . . . Three . . . Musk . . . ott . . . ers!*

They paused for a moment, bowed to each other, then came on again singing:

> We are the Otters,
> And modest far too long—
> It's high time Fame should spot us
> And lift us from the throng.

> Who are the gayest cavaliers?
> Who are the fighters Hildrok fears?
> Who are the lads that get the cheers?
>   *The . . . Three . . . Musk . . . ott . . . ers!*

The otters romped up to David and began shaking his hands vigorously.

'Congratulations, mate, on being rescued by us,' said Number One.

'Might ha' been some mumbling old chap like Badger,' giggled Number Two. 'Ain't you lucky it was us, David?'

'That jacket of yours has rather a pleasant taste,' said Number Three, reminiscently.

'That wasn't my jacket you could taste,' David told

him. 'It was *me*. Your teeth went right into my shoulder.'

'Indeed!' said Number Three. 'Hear that, you two young 'uns? Told you I'd got sharper teeth than you.'

'Garn! I don't believe it' (that was the giggler). 'Let's have a look,' and he ripped David's shirt open. 'Poo! And old Daddy Otter calls that a *bite*! Needs his teeth filing, he does!'

'I'll show you what a real bite is like,' growled Number Three, bowling him over, and David decided he'd better step in.

'Well, I wouldn't like to be bitten any harder than that,' he said. 'And thank you all for rescuing me. It was a magnificent effort and just in time because there was a great Wurg coming after me.'

That brought the otters round clamouring for more details and David had to tell them the whole story of his ordeal in the Pit of the Wurgs.

'So that's it,' he said finally. 'And now let's get back to Uncle Septimus. He'll want all the information I can give him . . .'

Number One cut in. 'Oh, no! That can't happen. *We'll* pass on all the information to the Captain. Because you won't be coming with us, see?'

'I certainly don't see!' David objected.

'You've got to go to Grunia, mate,' said the giggler.

'To help the people in the city with their defences,' added Number One.

The eldest otter shut them up sharply.

'It's this way,' he said to David. 'If Hildrok sees you with us, or if he learns you are with Captain Cobwebb, then he may carry out his threat to kill Toby. Until your brother has been rescued, Hildrok has got to think that your Uncle Septimus is doing nothing to interfere with his plans. So you've got to keep well away from us for the time being and Captain Cobwebb thinks it will be a good idea if you go and help the Grunians because they're in a terrible state of nerves. He says you don't *have* to go, because it's likely to prove a very dangerous journey, but . . .'

'Of course I'll go,' David answered. 'But I shall be worrying about Toby all the time.'

The otter drew him aside and whispered in his ear: 'The others don't know this, but Owl is already hidden inside Hildrok's fortress. He'll be working to free Toby and the boy Zillon.'

This news made David feel a good deal better and soon he and the eldest otter were going over the route he must take to avoid the territory where Hildrok and his Wurgs roamed and reach the city of Grunia.

'You'll be entirely on your own,' the otter told David, 'until you are about three miles outside the southern gate of the city. There you will come to a small cottage by the roadside. Go to the door and ask for a glass of water. When it's handed to you, at once throw the water on the earth instead of drinking it. By this sign Urb will know who you are and why you have come . . .'

'Who's this Urb?' demanded David. 'And how does he come into things?'

The otter glanced up at the sky. 'The light is dying,' he said, 'and you shouldn't delay. I will come with you a little way.' And he called to the others. 'Off you go, the two of you. Report to Captain Cobwebb and tell him we came across David unexpectedly and already he's on his way to Grunia. Clear off, now. I'll follow later.'

'What, all by yourself, Grandpa?' cried the giggler, racing off. And the other one called: 'So long, David. Any time you need rescuing, don't worry, we'll be there.'

'Cheek!' grunted the eldest otter.

'You said,' remarked David, thoughtfully, 'that you came across me unexpectedly. D'you mean that you hadn't actually come to this spot to rescue me?'

'Good heavens, no!' said the otter. 'It was Owl who went after you. We had orders to keep our eyes open in case any of you boys had escaped on your own and needed help. And if we found you we had certain things to tell you. But what we were after when we got hold of you was actually . . . was . . . something else.' He seemed rather embarrassed.

'Yes?' said David. 'Go on . . .'

'Well, you see,' answered the otter, not meeting David's eyes, 'we were ambling past this spot when we saw the earth move and we stopped and we sniffed and there was a . . . a . . . most appetising smell.'

'Do go on!' David urged.

The otter turned its head aside and wriggled its shoulders.

'Well, it's like this. There's only trout in the streams round here and we get a bit weary of it. Every day, you know, nothing but trout for every meal, awful! So when we smelt this . . .'

'Come on, tell the truth!' said David laughing. 'When you grabbed me and pulled me out you thought you'd got hold of a Wurg. And you have the nerve to call that "rescuing" me!'

'Well, we did pull you out, didn't we?' said the otter, ingratiatingly. 'And you aren't in there with the Wurgs any longer, are you? So that's a rescue, isn't it? Technically speaking, anyway.'

'And you'll all three go round swanking and patting yourselves on the back and shouting: *"We rescued David!"*'

'Oh, sure,' agreed the otter. 'Sure. We never miss a trick!'

'Well, I admire your cheek!'

'Oh, do you? I'm so pleased,' said the otter. 'Thank you, on behalf of the three of us, for such unstinted praise.'

David decided there was no answer to *that*, and with the otter leading the way they crossed the valley and came into the deep shade of a dense wood where their ways parted.

'You didn't answer one question I asked,' David reminded the otter as they said good-bye. 'This chap Urb— who is he? What's supposed to happen when I meet him? Do you know?'

'I know very little,' answered the otter. 'But I can tell you this. Urb is no man. And by the time you come out of that cottage, you'll have so many whiskers your own mother wouldn't know you. Ho-ho-ho!' chortled the otter. 'Cheerio!'

CHAPTER 12

ZILLON'S DARKEST HOUR

Toby tried and tried to work out some way of warning the owl about Hildrok's suspicions but the more he brooded on the problem the more his thoughts got in a tangle. At length he stood up and stretched himself.

'It's no good, Zillon,' he said. 'I'm not getting anywhere with this. Perhaps a bit of exercise will clear the fog out of my head. Don't forget that old Hildrok dumped a couple of hundred tree branches in the next room and he expects us to get them all trimmed, pronto. So come on, let's get down to it . . .' And Toby strode over to the door.

Before he could reach it Zillon had leaped in front of him.

'Toby, no!' he whispered fiercely. 'Don't touch that door—you'll be falling into Hildrok's trap! He told us he wanted the work done quickly, then he forgot to leave the door open so that we could go through and get on with it. If he comes back, as he will very soon, and finds us working in there then we shall have shown him that we know the secret of the doors.'

Toby was shaken. 'Thank goodness you stopped me, Zillon. I very nearly gave the show away,' he apologised.

'To watch Hildrok a man needs a hundred eyes,' said Zillon. 'He's as cunning as a fox. Let us just sit and wait for him. And when he comes watch out, for he will have some other trick in readiness to test us.'

As Zillon had foretold it was not long before the door swung back and Hildrok strode in. As the door closed behind him he marched across the room, apparently in a great rage.

'So! I return unexpectedly and find not a stroke of work has been done. You are here to serve me, not to sleep the days away! Out! Out! Get to work, if you do not want me to cast you into the Pit of Wurgs!' And Hildrok began to rain blows on their backs and push them towards the door.

This time it was Zillon who, through his terror of Hildrok, would have opened the door. But Toby, seeing the danger, suddenly dropped to his knees and as he raised his hands in supplication, Zillon went toppling over him.

'Please, oh please, Master!' cried Toby. 'Do not feed us to the Wurgs! Do not punish us! We wanted to do the work, Master, only the door was shut. We called for you but we could not make you hear. Open it for us, Master, and we will begin the work at once. We will work all night . . . we will . . .' And so Toby went burbling on until Hildrok grunted:

'Enough, enough! I had forgotten about the door,' he added, opening it. 'Get through and get on with the work I gave you. And do not stop until it is finished. Where do you think *you* are going?' he suddenly shouted at Zillon, who had started to turn back.

'My lamp, Master . . . the lamp . . .'

'Then don't stand wavering. Get it, fool! Get it!'

*　　*　　*

After Hildrok had closed both doors and left them alone they did not speak for a long time. Then Toby said: 'You were right, Zillon. We shall have to tread very cautiously where Hildrok is concerned.'

'Yes. I am ashamed of myself, Toby, for not seeing through his trick. But he frightened me so much that I found myself running to open the door. How he would have laughed!'

'Never mind. He didn't catch us out,' said Toby. 'I bet, you know, that if you'd not gone back for that lamp he would have left us in darkness in the other room just to test us again. Oh, I do NOT like old Scaly-Leg Duck-Feet!' declared Toby.

'Let's do the job as fast and as well as we can,' Zillon proposed. 'Quickly, because it will convince him that we fear him so much—and if he thinks *that*, he's less likely to believe we would ever dare to tamper with the doors. And if the task is well done also then that will please him. If he is pleased with us he may not watch us quite so closely. What do you think?'

'I think you should have been a *psychoplólogist*,' said Toby warmly, and Zillon beamed with joy because nobody had ever before praised him with such a big word.

So they buckled down to the task of trimming off sideshoots and cutting all the branches to the same size. It was not an easy job, the main reason being that the knives Hildrok had provided were not very sharp.

Zillon ran his thumb along the edge of his knife and grimaced at Toby. 'See how cautious Hildrok is!' he said. 'With a well-ground knife one could finish the job in half the time. But he takes no chances with us. A sharper knife might be dangerous—for him.'

Their arms and their backs were aching, and a huge pile of wood chips had grown beside them when at last, after some hours, they had finished preparing all the two hundred poles. They sat on the floor, leaning against the big rock table and wiped the sweat from their foreheads. It was then that Hildrok strode in. His great snake-like head swung angrily from side to side as he saw the two boys apparently lazing there on the floor but then his eyes found the neat, well-trimmed pile of poles. He was clearly surprised, pleasantly surprised.

'I see you have tried to please me,' he said in his grating voice. 'Continue to work like this and you have nothing to fear. Now I bring you the material for the next part of your task. But first move those chippings to your quarters, Zillon. They will make good firewood for you. Also, you will need much space in here for the next part of the task.'

When the room had been cleared Hildrok went into the outer corridor, leaving the door open, and his enormous claws began pitching into the room great piles of dry grass—so much that quite half of the space was packed with it from floor to ceiling. Last of all Hildrok threw down a large bundle of rope and turned to the two boys.

'Your next task will take longer, for it must be done very carefully. It will be sufficient if you have finished by the afternoon of tomorrow,' he said. 'You must take this grass and make it into large firm balls as wide across as you can stretch your arms sideways. Then you will fasten a ball on the end of each pole. Fasten it with a piece of rope and tie it securely—securely, mind: that is most important.'

Hildrok looked at them critically. 'You are weary. Do not start this work until you have eaten and rested. So that you may come in when you are ready, I will leave the door between this room and your quarters open for this night, Zillon. Remember, both of you: work as you have worked so far and all will be well. Fail me and you perish!'

Toby was looking first at the long poles and then at the pile of grass with a very puzzled expression. Hildrok saw it and began to laugh uproariously.

'You don't understand my secret weapon? Zillon will tell you that the walls of the city of Grunia are high and strong and cannot be climbed. Therefore the people think that they are safe from my ferocious Wurgs. But, imagine! Imagine two hundred Wurgs, each carrying one of these poles in its long tentacles. They swoop on the city walls and, nearing them they swerve. Then the Grunians see that the balls of grass are balls of fire! And, one after another, the Wurgs raise their powerful tentacles and hurl the blazing weapons high over the walls and into the city!

'I think that one attack will bring surrender. But if it needs a further lesson, then you will have to make me as many more of these weapons as are required—a thousand, if necessary. See to it that they are well fashioned, both of you!' And Hildrok left them.

'What can we do? What *can* we do?' cried Zillon.

'Make the things!' said Toby bitterly. 'We haven't any choice. And while we're making them let's keep thinking every second of every minute and trying to work out some method of getting out of here.'

'You don't know him as well as I do,' moaned Zillon despairingly. 'We shall never get the better of him. Didn't you notice, he said nothing about his hunt for that "white blackbird" as he called the owl? One day he will walk in here and throw its body on the floor, then ask us why we lied to him. And then . . . then . . . he'll feed us to the Wurgs!'

Zillon was almost hysterical and Toby saw that nothing could be done with him until the fit of despair had passed. He decided that the best thing was to ignore Zillon and go on with some work.

So he collected a great armful of grass and sat down to shape it into a ball. As he did so he felt something grip his finger, giving it a nasty pinch, and from the middle of the ball of grass a mocking voice declared:

'Poor little owl! One day Hildrok will walk in here and throw its body on the floor, will he? I thank you for your confidence in me, I do, indeed!' Toby snatched his finger away as the ball of grass began to roll about in the most alarming manner. Suddenly it burst apart, scattering bits all over the place and there, saucer-eyed, with wings angrily widespread, stood . . .

'Owl!' cried Toby. 'We didn't know how to warn you that Hildrok was hunting for you. I *am* glad to see you again.'

C

'*You* may be,' said the owl, acidly, 'but Weeping Willie there doesn't seem so sure about it. Fancy thinking that duck-footed monstrosity could catch me! Me, Owl, *Tyto alba alba*—one of the *Strigiformes* family, no less! Why, when he roamed up and down his tunnels hunting me I was flying silently behind him all the time! Laugh? I could have died! And to cap it all, he carried me in here himself, hidden in a bale of grass!'

'Owl, I think you're wonderful!' said Toby.

'I know, I know,' answered the owl, modestly, 'and I hope even Moping Monty there will admit it,' (and he gave Zillon a nasty look). 'I hope even he will have the grace to admit I'm wonderful when I tell you that I've worked out a plan for your escape.'

CHAPTER 13

WHAT DID THE BADGER MEAN?

DAVID would have been very much worried about what the otter had said would happen to him in the mysterious cottage if only the creature hadn't been so amused about it.

'I imagine he was getting his own back because I discovered that wonderful rescue was no rescue at all, really,' David told himself. All the same, it was a very puzzling prediction.

The route that the otter had pointed out to him now entered a dense forest. For a time the rays of a blazing sunset filtered through the dark columns of the trees and gave him light to distinguish the twists and turns of the track. Within an hour however, darkness fell and there was nothing to do but to rest and await the rising of the moon.

David did for a moment consider settling down for a complete night's sleep but he decided against it. Such a delay might mean his spending a second night in the forest and the otter had warned against this because it was so close to Hildrok's territory that some patrolling Wurg might be met with—or even the terrifying form of Hildrok himself.

He cast around for a comfortable spot in which he could curl up and which would afford him shelter from the heavy dew, for the temperature fell rapidly as daylight faded. He found a good place behind a thick clump of bushes—a sort of small cave beneath a projecting lip of rock into which eddying winds had driven a pile of fallen leaves.

David nestled into this warm bed and was very soon asleep. He woke refreshed, to see a thin streak of silver glinting through the clouds: it would not be long now before the moon was high. He wriggled and stretched his limbs and gave a couple of noisy yawns. And as he did so David's leafy bed began to heave and pitch so strongly he rolled right off on the hard earth, and . . .

'Fidget, fidget, fidget!' said a deep, slow voice, 'and they wonder why I likes to live on my own! Heaven knows how the rabbits get on. It's a marvel to me they manage to sleep at all, with dozens of 'em to a burrow.'

David, who had been very frightened at first, began to feel reassured. The voice wasn't an angry one. It might have been that of some old countryman discussing a spot of unpleasant weather.

'Tain't as if there was any real shortage of housing,' the voice rambled on. 'All an animal's got to do is make a hole, make it for himself and keep to himself, I say, and not wish his worrits and fidgets on other creatures . . .'

'I'm sorry, sir . . .' David began.

'. . . I say as every creature should have a place of his own,' went on the voice, ignoring him. 'But when I say that, *they* say t'aint traditional. They bin used to living together, in a bundle, like, ever since Old Daddy Noah packed us all in a boat, like sardines he did, and went a-cruising . . .'

'I didn't mean to disturb you,' (David managed to finish his apology at last) 'and I'll go away at once and leave you in peace.'

'Arr? you'm a well-spoken creature, indeed! Not many of 'em apologises. Generally they says "Oh, shut up, Badger, and stop mumbling," they says. You seem to be different. Let's have a look at you . . .'

And out of the leaves there emerged a broad muzzle with a white patch that stood out boldly in the growing moonlight. The badger regarded David steadily for a few moments then slowly shook its strong body free of its bedclothes.

'Arr, now,' it said. 'I've heard of you. You'll be Boy David, related to Captain Cobwebb. You just got away from Hildrok and you're on your way to help the human-kind in Grunia.'

David was astounded. 'But how could you possibly know that, Badger?' he asked.

'T'ain't, so wonderful I should know, if you think about it. Or rather, if you *takes time* to think, which no creatures seem to want to do these days. Look: when otters goes prancing and yelling about a thing all the way home, t'ain't surprising that the rabbits should hear 'em, is it? No? Right! Well, when rabbits hears any gossip at all, no matter what, they got to pass it on—just can't help themselves. So "*thump, thump, thump*" they goes with their hind feet 'till they've spelled out every word of the story. I tell you, Boy David, they'd like as not have shook me out of bed with the news if you hadn't bin lying a-top of me. So, you see,' added the badger, 'I know all about you going to help fight them Wurgs. What I don't know is how you reckon you're going to tackle 'em.'

'I'm afraid I don't know myself, yet,' said David. 'But I'm determined to find a way to beat them.'

'That's the way,' nodded the badger, appreciatively. 'You keep on thinking and, seeing how they say that two heads be better than one, why don't you tell me all you know about these Wurgs, and maybe I can put up an idea or two worth considering? You got the best part of half an hour afore full moon.'

So David described the Wurgs and the badger questioned him very closely about every point that he made. Finally the badger said: 'Right. Now the first thing that strikes me is the way these Wurgs move about. They stay close to the ground and they can't lift their big bodies over anything like a bush or a rock that's in their path. Seems to me the way they move themselves is by sucking in air and then blowing it out from under their bodies very fast, through lots of little tubes maybe. I reckon their ancestors were fish in the days when most of the world was covered in water and they got about like the octopus does today: sucking in water and blowing it out backwards. That's where the Wurgs got the trick from. But there's a difference, Boy David . . .'

Here the badger began to talk excitedly. 'If a fish stops pushing itself along it just stops moving. It don't sink, because it's floating in water. But the Wurgs move in air and you can't float in *that*. If they stop their engines, as you might say, they just flop. That's one thing. And here's another,' he went on, floundering somewhat and hesitating over his words. 'They have to stay close to the ground . . . so they have to *follow* the ground, don't you see, Boy?' The badger was almost talking to himself now, and in a very dreamy fashion.

'If it goes up, they goes up . . .' he murmured in a sing-song voice. '. . . and if it goes down, they goes down. And if . . . aha! . . . if . . . Oh, that's a very in-ter-est-ing spec-u-lation . . . oh, very . . .'

David broke in sharply: 'I beg your pardon, Badger, but I don't quite follow?'

'Oh, but you will.' The badger's voice got lower and lower and his words came more and more slowly. 'Just keep asking yourself: what happens then? How does it . . . if there isn't, I mean . . . ? Most interesting situation . . . *rrrrrrrrrr*.'

There was no doubt about it: the badger was asleep.

David found the track and strode away, angry with the badger and with himself for having wasted so much time listening to him. 'Old mumbler,' the otters had called him—and no wonder. All the same, David found that he could not get some of the badger's words out of his mind, crazy as they seemed to him.

He worked off his annoyance by keeping up as fast a pace as possible, hoping to get out of the deeper part of the forest, which was dangerously close to Hildrok's domain, while the moonlight held. He came to a place where the track snaked in a sharp bend between the great trunks of two mighty oaks and, as he slowed his pace to negotiate this, his ears caught a sudden movement ahead of him.

David flattened himself against one of the trees and waited. There was the sound again! Someone else was moving through the forest that night. Cautiously David peered out. A few yards down the track there was a wide clearing, white in the moonlight. As he looked there came a crackling of branches among the black shadows and a man stepped out and walked slowly to the centre of the clearing.

He wore a long cloak and the moonlight revealed nothing about him except that his hair was white. He stood there in absolute silence, clasping and unclasping his hands as if over-wrought.

Suddenly, with the soundless movement of a spectre, a gigantic figure leaped—it seemed from nowhere—and landed silently in front of the waiting man, towering over him, arms spread wide and steel talons gleaming. *Hildrok!*

The man fell to his knees in terror, hands over his eyes.

'Stand up and face me!' ordered Hildrok, and as the other at last stood, shaking, before him, he added silkily: 'I have come for your answer, my friend.'

'I will do anything you demand,' answered the man, in a low, trembling voice.

'Good,' said Hildrok. 'Your words carry much weight in the High Council of Grunia. You will speak to them as I direct you. You will persuade them to ask me for a truce, saying that my vengeance may be bought off with gold. Offer to come to me alone, to parley with me. At that meeting I shall tell you my terms for peace. Is that agreed?'

'Yes, yes. I have already promised. And when I have faithfully performed all you demand, you will not, Mighty Hildrok, forget your promise? You will be merciful and heed a father's prayer?'

And David almost cried out as he heard Hildrok's answer:

'When I have what I desire, Brindor, your eyes shall behold Zillon, your son.'

CHAPTER 14

A CRAZY CLIMB BY MOONLIGHT

ZILLON'S despair vanished as the owl uttered the word: 'Escape'.

'Owl, I am ashamed of myself,' he said. 'However could I have doubted that you are cleverer than Hildrok?'

70

'*I* never did,' said the owl. 'But you are young and still have much to learn. Would you care to do me a favour?'

'Anything, Owl, anything,' answered Zillon earnestly.

'Then kindly scratch my head while I tell you how you are both going to get out of here. Ah, thank you, Zillon, my boy . . . Oh, most stimulating! Now listen, the two of you . . .

'Down in the great cavern there is a door that leads into a short passage beside the Pit of the Wurgs. The door opens in the usual way. Behind it there is in the wall of the passage an iron ring and when this is turned the door of the great cavern is lifted up. It stays open for some minutes, then it falls back into place. There must be some way of opening the door from the outside when Hildrok brings back his Wurgs at dawn after raiding your people's cattle, Zillon. But *we* don't intend to come back!'

Toby said: 'That's marvellous, Owl. Only . . . how do we get down into the great cavern? We can't climb down. It's too high to jump, and we can't fly, you know.'

'I know, I know,' replied the owl, testily. 'You are two sad cases of arrested development. Perhaps in a few thousand years you may manage to grow feathers. However, we must deal with things as they are. And since you can't fly and it's too dangerous for you to try to climb down or to jump, then you'll just have to slide down the rope that Hildrok has so kindly provided, won't you?'

'Owl, I *said* you were wonderful!' cried Toby. 'Come on, Zillon, let's get the rope in place.'

They struck a snag right away. Hildrok's hank of sturdy rope was quite long enough to reach from the edge of the rock-face to the ground, but they could find no projecting lump of rock to which they could fasten the top end.

'Then we must wedge it under the door of our room,' Zillon suggested. 'But how?'

'Knot the rope round one of the knives Hildrok provided us with,' said Toby. 'Pass the rope under the door and close the door as we leave. The knife can't slip through and the rope will be held firmly.'

They measured the rope out and they now found that when they went down it into the cavern they would have to drop the last ten to twelve feet.

'Think you can manage that?' Toby asked and as Zillon nodded the owl broke in.

'Then come along, come along! Don't forget the other

knife, Boy Toby. You may need it to defend yourselves if we run into Hildrok or some prowling Wurg. Bring your lamp, Zillon. I don't need its light, but you do.'

The door of rock closed behind them, holding the escape-rope firmly, and they hurried down the corridor. Zillon blew out his light and clambered down the rope, taking the drop with ease, and then re-lit the lamp for Toby's descent.

With the owl fluttering around excitedly they were soon through the other door and reaching for the iron ring. It took the combined strength of the two boys to turn it . . . slowly . . . slowly. But suddenly the ring moved easily and they heard a strange rushing sound behind the rock-face.

'Look!' Zillon shouted.

For, like a huge curtain, the vast slab of rock that closed the end of the great cavern was sliding upwards. Outside the cavern moonlight, bright as day, shone down on rocks and trees and the fugitives could hear the music of mountain streams.

The two boys dashed out under the starry sky and began to dance around for sheer joy, while the owl sat on a rock and let them have their heads for a few moments. At length the owl called:

'That will do. We must get on our way.'

'Which way do we go?' asked Toby. 'To see Captain Cobwebb?'

'I'm not sure yet,' answered the owl. 'He may have other instructions for us. With Hildrok and his Wurgs roaming about all over the place it will be dangerous to travel at night at the lower levels, across open country and amid pastures and isolated farms. That is where the cattle are and therefore where the Wurgs are hunting. No, my proposal is that we go upwards, right to the top of this great mountain of rock. There we'll be safe from our enemies and you can rest while I call for news and for orders.'

'What, climb *this*?' Toby pointed up at the sheer cliff face behind him in dismay.

'Oh, if only you could fly! If only you weren't such inefficient creatures!' sighed the owl. 'Follow me. I will show you a place where even you can mount—given a little courage . . .'

And as the owl moved silently ahead like a white

ghost, the two boys followed, with just one comment, from Zillon: 'I don't know how much *courage* I've got, Toby, but I've got enough fear of Hildrok to make me risk anything to escape from him.'

A sudden roar and a crash from behind told them that the huge rock door of Hildrok's fortress had fallen back into place: They hurried on.

'This is the spot,' said the owl at last. 'The rock seems to have been forced up in layers and there are ridges that run across the surface. Also you will see that shrubs and small trees have been able to gain a foothold. Are you prepared to try it? I will fly beside you and point out the way.'

Toby looked up and Zillon looked up and they both felt cold and sick inside. But . . .

'It's got to be done,' said Toby, 'so here goes. And don't look down, Zillon.'

The two boys will never forget that climb. Pressed close to the rock-face, and straining their eyes upwards all the time, they sought for footholds as the owl instructed and reached for branches or the matted roots of shrubs to pull themselves to higher ledges. Many times loose gravel gave way beneath their feet and cascaded in a pattering rain down the rock-face. More than once their weight tore a shrub out by its roots and the climber found himself suspended over space by one hand and a slipping toe-hold.

And the agony went on. It went on for almost three hours, by which time clouds were beginning to pack around the moon and wisps of grey mist floated along the rock-face until at times they could scarcely see the ledges to which they clung.

But at length they reached the top and heaved themselves, panting, on to an enormous boulder-strewn plateau of rock. Before them a wide pool palely mirrored the moon and shifting clouds through a veil of mist. They crawled well away from the edge of the mountain and lay with outspread limbs, sobbing for breath.

'Well done! Well done!' declared the owl, marching backwards and forwards with his funny rolling step. 'But what an expenditure of energy just to raise yourselves a thousand feet! Why, I could fly a thousand *miles* without exhausting myself like that. But I suppose,' he added, 'that we higher animals shouldn't be too critical of the less developed creatures. Rest yourselves. Rest yourselves. And kindly remain quiet while I communicate.'

And the owl fluffed out the feathers round his neck, closed his great round eyes until they were only pin-points, and began to hoot softly. At length he stopped and although his voice was quite low and gentle the boys could hear his hoots drifting far away in the darkness long after he had finished.

'Listen to the echoes!' said Zillon.

'Relay stations, stupid!' replied the owl, irritably. 'Not echoes. And I thought I told you to remain quiet. Listen!'

And now, distantly, there came faint hooting in reply, which grew louder and louder as the message was passed from owl to owl in their direction. At last the hooting ceased.

'Well, well,' declared the owl. 'That *is* news indeed! Boy Toby, your brother *did* escape and is on his way to Grunia at Captain Cobwebb's request to help them defend their city against Hildrok. You and Zillon are to go there also. But first you must go, as speedily as possible, and seek the road that enters the city of Grunia from the south. About three miles from the city gate you will come to a small cottage by the roadside. Go to the door and ask for a glass of water. When it is handed to you, throw the water on the ground at once, instead of drinking it. By this sign Urb will know who you are and why you have come. End of message.'

'Urb, Urb? Who's he?' demanded Toby.

But Zillon, with a cry, had leaped to his feet and with shining eyes was shaking Toby by the shoulder.

'Urb is not a man, Toby!' he almost shouted. 'Urb is the Wise Woman of Grunia. What do you think of *that*!'

CHAPTER 15

MORE THRILLS BY MOONLIGHT

'I DON'T know what to think,' replied Toby, absently. 'Perhaps the Wise Woman wants to give us another prophecy. Anyhow, I expect we'll find out what it's all about when we get there. There's something, here and now, that interests me much more. Come, Zillon, and see.'

He walked Zillon along the edge of the pool.

'Look,' said Toby, 'where water runs out of the pool here. This isn't a natural overflow—there's a channel been cut into the rock and cut deeply, so there's always water in it. There are two or three more further along, but let's follow this one.'

The water-filled channel ran for about fifty yards and ended at a round hole, full to the brim. The owl said: 'Just a minute. I'll inspect the others. I can do it quicker than you can,' and he took off and flew rapidly around, a flitting white shadow in the moonlight.

'They're all the same, Boy Toby,' said the owl on his return. 'Every water channel ends in a hole, and the hole's full of water. Does it mean anything to you?'

Zillon recalled: 'There was a small pipe of wood in the wall of my quarters and when I drew out a plug I could get a little water for drinking. Perhaps it came from here.'

'But not all those channels of water are needed to give you a few drips from a tiny tap,' the owl pointed out. 'And they all lead to different points.'

'If there was a tap under any one of those places,' Toby mused, 'and you turned it on why, you'd be flooded out before you knew where you were.'

'Why so quickly?' asked the owl. 'I don't quite see . . .?'

'Because of the pressure of the water, falling from such a terrific height,' explained Zillon. '*Why, yes, of course . . . !*'

'THE DOORS!' shouted Toby and Zillon together. 'It works the doors in Hildrok's caverns!'

'Remember the rushing noise behind the rock when we were turning the iron ring to open the door of the great cavern so we could get out?' said Zillon. 'It was water falling from here that worked the machinery.'

'Yes,' said Toby. 'Just think. If only we could pipe the water out of this pool, we could seal up Hildrok and the Wurgs for ever!'

'It's a brilliant idea,' said the owl, drily. 'But even if you had a pipe it would take ages to empty that pool, even if there was no rain. And I might say, young fellow, that at this height it rains two nights out of every three.'

'All the same, I wish . . .' began Toby.

'All the same, you've had your orders,' replied the owl

75

sternly, 'and those are to go by the house of Urb and on to Grunia. Don't you want to see your brother?'

'Of course I do.'

'Then get moving,' answered Owl. 'That's the direction. You'll be walking on rock like this for about a mile. Then the ground begins to dip sharply and you'll find yourselves sliding on shale, with just a few big trees here and there. After that the way is easier and leads to a well-trodden track through a patch of forest to the road.'

'But aren't you coming with us, Owl?' asked Zillon.

'No,' said the owl. 'I've got orders, too. But don't worry. I'll be seeing you!' And, like a gentle puff of white smoke, he was gone.

So the two boys strode out towards distant Grunia. The night was bitterly cold but by the time they reached the dizzy slopes of loose shale they were perspiring heavily. And by the time they had worked their slow way across them they were aching in every limb, for at each step the earth slid beneath their feet and they felt themselves constantly in danger of hurtling in an avalanche of stones to certain death a thousand feet below.

But at last they came into the forest and as soon as they reached a clearing they flopped down among the mossy roots of a great tree, leaned against its trunk and heaved a long, long sigh of relief.

Neither of them spoke for some time. Then Zillon said:

'D'you know what?'

'No. What?'

'I wish I had Owl's wings!'

'I'll wish something better than that.'

'What?'

'I wish Owl had my feet!'

A long silence.

'I say, Toby.'

'Mmmm?'

'Isn't it surprising how much you can see when your eyes get used to the darkness?'

'Is it? Surprise me, then! What can you see?'

'Well. Look where I'm pointing. Fireflies!'

'Fireflies? Oh, I see. Mmm. Aren't they a bit big for fireflies?'

76

'Are they?'

'I think so. Besides, I don't think fireflies glow red . . .'

'Well, if they're not fireflies, what are they?'

'Let's go over and have a look.'

Toby and Zillon creaked to their feet, and as they did so the moon floated out from behind a cloud into a clear patch of sky. Every bush and tree and leaf along the forest path ahead sprang out as clear as day.

And there, surging towards the two boys, red eyes blazing, fangs dripping, was—

'A Wurg!'

As they cried together that terrible word, Toby and Zillon turned and dashed headlong back, trying to put the trunk of the great tree between themselves and the monster.

They were too late.

With a snarl that shook the forest, the huge beast flung itself at them.

Toby tripped, and, twisting as he fell, found himself on his back gazing up into the cavernous mouth of the Wurg.

And then, from the black shadows behind the monster there came a deep grunt, and a flying form of fur and fury hurtled into the moonlight. With a flash of white teeth, steely jaws closed on the Wurg's stubby tail. Raising itself on its haunches, the newcomer—whatever it was— gave a powerful jerk of its head to one side and then let go. Toby's attacker, thrown off course, shot past him and crashed head first into the tree trunk.

The Wurg dropped to the ground like a stone. Its red eyes flickered for a second, then closed. Its weaving tentacles drooped and streamed across the ground like wet, black ribbons.

And as Toby and Zillon slowly got to their feet a deep, rather lazy voice said pensively:

'Arr! There you are, now. I 'member sitting one day and speculating what I'd do if ever I come across one o' they Wurgs. I said: "*I'd get him by his little bitty tail, that's what I'd do—and swing his wicked head agin a tree.*" And how they rabbits laughed at me!' "*Old Daddy Badger, day-dreaming again,*" they said. And I said to them, I said, "'*Tis a wise thing to day-dream because dreams is apt to come true—specially bad ones—and if you ain't dreamed what to do when that happens, then*

The Badger day-dreaming. "'Tis a wise thing to do," he always said, "because dreams is apt to come true—especially bad ones—and if you ain't dreamed what to do when that happens, then where are you?"

where are you?" Well, like as not I'd have been in a Wurg's stomach . . .'

Toby said: 'And you saved *us* from being in a Wurg's stomach too, Badger! Thank you for saving our lives.'

There was a moment's silence as the badger shuffled forward and rather shortsightedly lifted his dark muzzle with the white patch to look into Toby's face.

'You know,' said the badger, 'you'm the second well-spoken boy I met around these parts. From what I seen o' boys I didn't think I'd ever come across even one that'd speak a creature fair. 'Tis a pleasant surprise. This first boy was kin to our Captain Cobwebb and Boy David was his name . . .'

'And this is his brother, Toby!' burst out Zillon.

'Well met then, indeed,' said the badger. 'I heard Owl passing some news along tonight. You speak like a Grunian, so I reckon you'll be the Zillon that got away from Hildrok's fortress with Boy Toby here. You're aiming to meet Boy David in Grunia?'

'That's right,' said Toby, 'and thanks to you, Badger, we'll soon be there.'

'Arr, you won't though,' answered the badger. 'Not at the rate you was travelling, you won't be—not in time at any rate.'

Just at that moment there was a deep kind of sigh from the Wurg. A ripple ran along its limp tentacles.

'Look out!' yelled Zillon. 'It's not dead!'

'Don't you worry,' said the badger, as the boys turned to flee. 'I can handle such as he.' And he ambled to the Wurg and squatted on top of its wide back, near the head.

Slowly the lid of one eye began to lift and the Wurg directed a red stare up at the badger. The badger raised one big forepaw and brought it heavily down on the Wurg's eyelid. The monster shuddered with pain and the red glare vanished.

'He's got a headache, see,' said the badger, 'so he's very tender round the eyes. Just give him a smart tap there now and then and he'll be a very docile animal. That's an idea I worked out one time when I was a-day-dreaming,' mused the badger, '—how I could make an old Wurg into a useful creature like the rest of us be, in our different ways. And if you young fellows will be patient with Old Badger, for a moment or two, I'll show you how it's done. Now just get me a stout piece o' wood, will 'ee, Boy Toby?'

Toby ferreted around and came back with a strong branch about three feet long. The badger, from his perch on the Wurg's head, gave instructions.

'Shove it between his teeth. Push it right back, now. That's the way. Now, boys. Each of you take hold of a tentacle. Knot it once round the end of the wood. Take the ends of the tentacles and knot 'em together firmly. Wurg can't do anything dangerous with them tentacles now they'm knotted. Them's the reins for you to drive him with. He'll carry two of you. Come on. Who's going to do the steering?'

To tell the truth, neither Toby nor Zillon was very keen to get on the back of a Wurg, but the badger was so matter-of-fact about it, and they had seen how well his day-dreaming had served him when he did battle with the monster, that they couldn't very well refuse.

As to the 'steering' as the badger called it . . . Toby told Zillon: 'If we go driving into Grunia with a Grunian holding the reins, it'll remind people of the prophecy and give them courage to face Hildrok's big attack.'

'But you were the first to ride on a Wurg,' objected Zillon. 'It's you who fulfilled the prophecy.'

'I wasn't *riding* it,' grinned Toby. 'I was lashed down to it. Also, no Grunians saw me and I'm not a native of your country anyway. It'll have a lot more effect if *you* sail through the city gates holding the reins.'

So it was agreed.

'Now the trick is this,' said the badger as Zillon prepared to mount. 'Put your feet well apart and have the big toe of each foot right over each of his eyes. One little tap on his eyelid will keep him obedient.'

Zillon took the reins. Toby stood behind him, hands on his shoulders, and with a flick of his wrist Zillon edged the Wurg around until it faced along the track that led to the high road and Grunia.

Once again they thanked the badger and were raising their hands to wave farewell when he halted them.

'I just remembered,' he mumbled. 'I had a long talk with that Boy David and I was a-working something out in my mind that I wanted to tell him. Well, I didn't get it worked out afore he had to leave me. Now, dang me, I got the solution to the problem in my mind. But I can't remember what that problem was!

'Anyway, just you tell Boy David when you sees him that Old Badger says *when it stops, they drops*. That's the answer, tell him. Though I can't remember *what* it's the answer *to* . . .' said the badger.

Zillon jerked the reins. The boys waved good-bye, the Wurg moved off down the track, quickly picking up speed.

And the badger's voice followed them, faintly asserting his conviction:

'*When it stops, they drops*, tell him. That's the answer, all right.'

CHAPTER 16

<h2 style="text-align:center">TREASON IN THE FOREST</h2>

'*When I have what I desire, Brindor, your eyes shall behold Zillon, your son.*'

Hildrok's ugly claws clasped the shoulder of Zillon's father and tightened until the man cried out.

'Such pain will be only the beginning of Zillon's suffering if you fail me,' said Hildrok, releasing him. 'You have two days in which to persuade the High Council to seek a treaty. After that I will wait no longer, but attack!' And Hildrok was gone.

Brindor stood for a few minutes motionless, his head sunk on his chest, one hand clutching his aching shoulder. Then, with a sob, he plunged into the shadows and vanished.

What a foul trick it was for Hildrok to threaten Zillon's life unless his father persuaded the Grunians to accept defeat—because that was what Hildrok really intended. Once the gates of Grunia were opened to him David was sure that Hildrok would sweep in at the head of his rapacious Wurgs and the city and all within it would be destroyed. And David was certain, neither Brindor nor Zillon would be spared.

There were only two days left in which to foil that plan, so the sooner he could do something about it the better.

David made a quick decision. Brindor would obviously make his way back to the city as quickly as possible and, since he was a Grunian, he would know the shortest route through the forest.

David left the track, hurried across the clearing to the point where he had seen Zillon's father disappear. Sure enough, behind the bushes he came upon a wavering path that seemed to run in the right direction and he set out upon it as fast as he could go. It was not very long before he heard the sound of footsteps ahead and after that David cautiously kept his distance until he saw a black figure descending a long slope to meet the moonlit road. David turned quickly at right angles and came out on the road some distance behind his quarry.

As quietly as possible he overhauled Brindor and then, when only a few paces behind him, he quickened his steps, whistling gaily as he did so.

Brindor swung round with a startled cry.

'Boy! Hey, you . . .' he called as David came level with him. 'Come here! This is no time for one so young to be upon the high road. What business have you here?'

David made as if to push past him.

'The best business in the world,' he said. 'I go to tell the High Council of Grunia of a plot by Hildrok the Wurgmaster.'

Brindor seized his arm.

'And how would a child like you know what is in Hildrok's mind?' he asked. He laughed, but David could sense the fear behind his words.

'One who knows it well has told me,' answered David. 'There is a man whose voice is powerful in the High Council. There is a boy whose life is in Hildrok's hands. Hildrok plans to blackmail the man: the boy's life in return for the man's treason to his country.'

There was a long silence.

At last Brindor said: 'Who is this man?'

'I do not know his name.'

'And the boy?'

'I do not know his name either.'

Brindor seeemed much relieved. 'I should not advise you to go before the High Council with such a cock-and-bull story,' he said. 'Without names it means nothing, nothing.'

'Oh,' said David. 'I can give them the name of the

person who told me what Hildrok plans to do. It is Zillon.'

'Zillon!' Brindor started, then tried to recover his casual tone. 'And who is he, and when and where did he tell you these things?' he asked.

'He also is a prisoner of Hildrok,' answered David, 'but as to when and where I heard this from him, I will not say.'

Brindor was silent for a time. Then he asked softly: 'This Zillon . . . did he say any more about this, this boy?'

David said: 'Only that the boy says he would rather Hildrok killed him than that his father should buy his life by selling his country.'

Brindor sighed deeply. Then he halted and turning put his hands on David's shoulders and looked into his eyes.

'I, too, am a member of the High Council,' he said. 'I know the man you speak of, and I will tell him all you have told me. His son will have no cause to be disappointed in him. He will never advise surrender, come what may. Will you trust me in this, friend of Zillon?'

And when Brindor spoke like this David knew his message had got through. He nodded.

'Then let us hasten,' said Brindor, quickening his pace, 'for we have some miles to go and the High Council meet soon after dawn.'

But David excused himself on the grounds that he needed to rest a while and was now in no hurry. He sat down beside the road and watched Brindor stride along until he was out of sight. Then he set off for the cottage of Urb.

*   *   *

The cottage stood by the roadside, surrounded by a white-painted fence. The roof was of heavy thatch and the windows were small. A plume of blue wood-smoke rising from the squat chimney, together with a mouth-watering smell of cooking, showed that someone was busy inside. David opened the gate and walked up the flagged path to the door. Beside it on the wall there was a notice in a rough wooden frame. It had been written by hand, the ink was faded, and whoever had done it had tried to cram in so much information that David had to push his nose against the glass and screw up his eyes to make out the words. This is what it said:

THE ONLY ORIGINAL
URB
WISE WOMAN OF GRUNIA
Prophecies Grim & Gay Our
Speciality.
Patronised by the High Council
of Grunia: Terms on Application.

. . .

Hands Read: : Bumps Felt: : Stars
Consulted: : Tea-Leaves Deciphered: :
By the Hour or Minute: : Lowest Rates: :
Children Half-price: : Big Discounts on
Last Season's Charms.

. . .

Pills: : Potions: : Herbal Remedies
(Made Under Supervision of Accredited Wizard).
Snacks: : Lunches: : Cream Teas: : Bird-Seed: :
Fertiliser: : Scissors Ground: : Swords
Honed and polished: : Corn-Plasters and Buttons.

'Well, this seems to be a regular old junk-shop,' David told himself. However, he had Captain Cobwebb's orders. So he lifted the heavy iron knocker and banged on the door. After a moment or so it opened a few inches and a little old man with steel-rimmed spectacles and no teeth peered round the edge of the door and stared at him without a word.

'Please, sir,' said David politely, 'could you oblige by giving me a glass of water? I have walked a long way and I'm very thirsty.'

The face vanished and after a few minutes returned. A gnarled hand, holding a cup of water, was thrust towards David.

He thanked the old man and lifted the cup. And then he paused, for he thought to himself: 'I'm about to do the silliest thing I've ever done in my life—and if that kind old man were to hit me right on the jaw for it, it would be no more than I deserve. Still, I've been told I must do it, so here goes . . .' And he turned the cup upside down and spilled out every drop of water.

At once the door was flung wide and the old man (who may have been small but, as David now saw, was enormously wide, with arms like great hams), cried: 'Come in, good sir. We have been expecting you. Urb, my wise little chicken!' he called, 'here is Captain Cobwebb's nephew come to be fitted for his new position. This way, sir.' And he hustled David through another door into the presence of Urb, Wise Woman of Grunia.

Urb must have been, without doubt, the biggest, fattest woman in the world, the most colourful and, maybe, the merriest. Her vast bulk almost hid the enormous, high-backed oak chair in which she sat beside the fire, one arm outstretched and holding a great copper ladle with which she was stirring soup in a black iron cauldron that hung over the blazing logs. Her voluminous gown of silk blazed with barbaric colours. Her teeth gleamed white, her bold black eyes flashed in the firelight. Black corkscrew curls framed her face and danced on her shoulders and her head was covered by a silken scarf of blinding kingfisher-blue.

Despite Urb's colourful appearance, however, there was something strong enough to draw David's attention elsewhere, and that was the black iron cooking-pot and the smell that came from it. Even as he tried to murmur a greeting to the Wise Woman his quivering nose was pointed to the pot. (You just can't have any idea how hungry he was.)

And then, with one glance at him, Urb said something that made David decide on the spot that she was indeed the wisest woman he'd ever met.

'Husband!' she called. 'A bowl of soup for the boy; he's starving. Let him take that while I prepare a meal. And after that—I swear, my bright young warrior, I'll turn you into the most fearsome General that ever led an army!'

CHAPTER 17

THE MAKING OF GENERAL DZONG

DAVID will remember that meal with pleasure for as long as he lives; but he will always be thankful that he had eaten it before he was told the Grunian names of the things that made up the various dishes.

To begin with, he had a steaming bowl of Blood Apple Soup. Then came Thigh Flesh From Pup of Curly-Coated Mountain Grass-Eater, accompanied by Crying-Juice Bulbs, Diced Red Dagger-Roots and Sweet Seeds of Green-Purse Vine.

And finally he was served a steaming ball of Hard-Fat and Powdered Grains Dough, absolutely streaming with Humming-Fly Nectar.

David has since said—very often—that the nearest anybody could get to a meal like that in England (although of course it could never have been half as appetising as the Grunian menu) would be Tomato Soup; Leg of Welsh Lamb with Onions, Carrots and Peas; with Suet Pudding and Treacle to follow.

At length David sat back in a comfortable chair before the blazing fire, with a steaming mug of Grunian Ko-Ko in his hand, and summoned up enough courage to ask Urb something that had worried him ever since he'd read the notice on the door outside: how was it that a Wise Woman who made prophecies and was famed throughout Grunia should bother with such paltry things as reading people's palms, selling charms, providing snacks and grinding scissors?

'Why, bless your heart, lad,' cried the Wise Woman, with a laugh that set all her five chins quivering, 'it's because fame and money are two different things entirely! I might take ten years to think up a good prophecy, see. And it might take ten years more—or maybe fifty—before it comes true. And until it comes true how can people tell whether you're a good prophesier or not? So you see, people who want a prophecy have to buy it without knowing whether they'll get value for their money.

So they don't want to pay much. You can understand that, can't you?'

'Yes,' said David, thoughtfully. 'I hadn't thought of it that way.'

'When the High Council of Grunia came to me and wanted a real good, optimistic prophecy about Wurgs, I worked hard and I came out with a beauty—you know, about a child riding by on the back of one of them monsters. But they hummed and hawed about payment, they did, and in the end all I got out of 'em was free firewood for a month, a brace of fowl, and a pewter teapot with the handle broke off, from the Town Hall canteen. Sad, isn't it?'

'Yes, it makes life very hard. I can see that,' said David.

'It would if I let it,' replied Urb, with another big laugh. 'But I don't let it, David. You take heed o' me: don't bother about big prophecies that you can sell only once in a lifetime. Small Prophecies and Quick Returns, that's my motto: make a lot o' little prophecies that you can sell to hundreds of people every week. You should see my Astrology Clinic, boy—three nights a week and packed out! Cash on the nail, too. "*Cross me palm with silver*" I says and then I read tomorrow's fortune in their hands ... "*This may be your lucky day ... A dark man seems to be showing interest in your career ... Do not sign any papers without seeking advice ... Next please!*" It's money for jam!'

'And that,' declared Urb, 'is enough o' *that*, because now we've got to get down to the job of making you look stern enough and old enough and big enough to command obedience from the High Council of Grunia. They've had a letter from Captain Cobwebb, as head of a friendly country, to say he's sending that great soldier General Dzong to help 'em defend themselves against Hildrok, so they'll be expecting you.

'Husband! Bring me the wig and the beard and the costume and let's begin ...'

*　　*　　*

For the next hour the two of them worked on David's appearance and, as he watched the changes in the big mirror they placed before him, he saw his own features vanishing bit by bit and a strange, fierce figure beginning to replace them.

To begin with. Urb fitted on his head something like a flesh-coloured bowler hat without a brim which had the effect of making his face seem twice as long. On top of his new head was fitted a heavy wig of thick, curling iron-grey hair. This was carried down his cheeks and across his chin, from which it stuck out, a foot wide and a foot deep. A massive moustache covered his upper lip, its ends curled and pomaded into stiff spikes that stood out on each side of his face. Big, bristling brows were stuck above his eyes and one eye covered by a black patch, pierced with a number of tiny holes that enabled him to see perfectly. Then David was squeezed into a tight-waisted blue jacket covered in gold lace, white buckskin breeches, and shining black leggings from knee to ankle. His boots were fitted with hidden platform soles that increased his height by a good four inches. Finally Urb hung over one of David's shoulders a crimson cape with a blue silk lining, pressed on his head a military hat, decorated with the emblem of a fierce eagle in gold, and with a peak that lay flat against his brow. Finally she thrust into his hand a long sword with a jewelled scabbard.

'Anything missing?' she said. 'Ah yes . . . medals.' And when these were pinned on David's breast, Urb stood back and surveyed her handiwork.

'That'll do,' she said. 'From now on you're General Dzong, the *great* General Dzong. Don't forget it and don't let the Grunians forget it. Remember, they're only simple farming folk. They've never had an army and they've never known anything but peace until now. Right? Any problems?'

'Yes,' said David weakly. 'I don't know whether I can walk in these boots!'

So Urb and her husband took his arms and they marched him up and down until he got the feel of the things. Then Urb had him practising a military walk, clicking his heels, and saluting.

And just as she had told David she was satisfied with his progress, there was a knock at the outer door. Then there were voices, some coming and going, and finally the excited voice of Urb's husband: 'Come in, come in! Urb, my little chicken, the two others have arrived!'

This is what the great soldier General Dzong looked like when Urb, the Wise Woman of Grunia, had finished kitting him out. Walking in those high-heeled boots was quite a feat.

David stood, tall, stern and forbidding beside Urb. Two boys entered the room, looking weary and bemused. They came forward uncertainly.

David suddenly barked in a loud military voice.

'Attention, you slovenly louts! Stand to attention and salute when you meet an officer!'

They nearly jumped out of their shoes and their jaws dropped at the sight of that fierce face.

Then Zillon slowly brought one hand up to his mop of red hair in a clumsy salute.

Toby, whose glasses had steamed up in the heat of the room, removed them, wiped them with his handkerchief, then taking a couple of steps forward, he raised them to peer at the glowering officer before him.

Then, very deliberately, Toby raised his right hand . . . and jabbed him in the stomach. General Dzong folded up like a pocket knife.

'*David, you fathead!*' cried Toby. '*I'd have known you anywhere.*'

It was only when the uproar and the laughter had died down a bit that Urb and the boys became aware of the antics of Urb's husband. He was dancing about, beckoning to Urb and then pointing to the outer door.

Zillon was the first to realise what all the fuss was about.

'Oh, I'm sorry. Urb,' he said. 'We left our steed outside, is that all right?'

They all crowded to the front door and out into the garden.

And there, hitched to the fence post, panting slightly and undulating close to the ground was—a Wurg.

Urb gave one incredulous look. Then she let out a shriek that shook the birds' nests out of the thatched roof.

'Heavens above! Me prophecy's come true!' she cried. And fainted right away on the doorstep.

CHAPTER 18

TWO MYSTERIOUS STEEDS

It took all four of them quite some time to heave the Wise Woman back into the cottage and plonk her down in her big chair by the fire, where she sprawled, breathing heavily and with a wide, happy smile.

'What can we do to bring her round?' demanded Toby.

'Leave her to me, young sir,' said the husband and, reaching up to a box of turkey feathers that stood on the mantelshelf, he took one and pushed the end into the fire. Then he thrust it, crackling and fuming, under Urb's nose.

'Ugh!' sniffed Zillon. 'What a smell. I think the cure's worse than the ailment . . .'

But it worked, and very quickly, for Urb wrinkled her big nose, gave a sudden mighty sneeze, and sat up.

'Is it true?' she demanded. 'Is there really a Wurg out there, tied up like a horse?'

'There is indeed, ma'am,' answered Zillon, 'and I and my friend Toby rode here on its back from the forest.'

'Zillon held the reins,' put in Toby modestly. 'I just hung on to *him*.'

'But how on earth did you tame the monster?' asked David.

'Oh,' said Toby, 'Badger taught us how to do that.'

Urb put in: 'Hold! No more until you have eaten. Good tales come easier with a full stomach.'

So the two Wurg-riders ate and ate and ate until Zillon sighed and pushed his plate away and even Toby could manage only three more helpings of Hard-Fat and Powdered-Grains Dough, even though it was smothered in Humming-Fly Nectar, of which he is extremely fond.

'And now,' said Urb, 'let us hear all about your escape and about the badger's part in this Wurg-riding business.'

When the story had been told David remarked: 'I had quite a session with Badger myself, but I can't say he helped me very much.' And he told them how Badger had tried to work out a way to defeat the Wurgs.

As he finished his story Zillon burst out: 'Thank heaven you told us this, for I had almost forgotten! Badger spoke of it to us.'

'Yes, and he gave us a message for you,' Toby said. 'He said he'd forgotten what problem it was he'd been talking to you, but he'd just found the solution. I'll tell you his *exact* words . . .'

Toby scratched his head to stimulate his memory and he pondered a while, then he said:

'Badger's orders were: "Just you tell Boy David that Old Badger says *when it stops, they drops*. That's the answer, tell him. *When it stops, they drops*. That's the answer, all right!"'

They all turned to stare at David.

'*Is* that the answer?' asked Zillon. 'Do you know now how to beat the Wurgs, David?'

David threw up his hands. 'I've no more idea about what Badger means than I had before,' he said despairingly.

'So what are you going to do, then?' asked Urb, looking at him sharply.

'I'll keep on thinking about it until tomorrow morning— because I'll have had a chance to look around the city by then and talk with the High Council, and something may come out of that to give me a clue as to what Badger is driving at. If it hasn't, then I'll have to think up some plan of my own, because Hildrok will attack the city that night.'

'Oh, will he? How did you learn that?' asked Urb swiftly.

David saw that he was in danger of having the matter of Brindor's talk with Hildrok wrested from him if he were not careful. He had no intention of letting anyone, Zillon most of all, know how near the boy's father had been betraying his country, so he simply said 'I wish I could tell you, ma'am, but I dare not put my informant in danger by revealing his name.'

'Reg'lar military mind the boy's got, hasn't he, husband?' grinned the Wise Woman with a wink.

'And a wise one,' agreed the husband, 'since he's decided to think so long and hard about what Badger said. A knowing animal, Badger. Keep his words in mind, boy. You may see light sooner than you imagine.'

Urb said: 'He's right. But let our General Dzong get himself to the city as soon as possible and put some heart into the people. And let his brother here go with him, while Zillon follows after on the Wurg.'

'But why shouldn't we all go together?' asked Zillon.

'You may do as you wish,' said Urb, 'because the future of Grunia rests with the three of you and you must decide for yourselves what way is best. But before you do so, listen to my suggestions. First: the Grunians will be impressed to have the help of a General sent to them by Captain Cobwebb. But they will have even better heart for battle if they find that Captain Cobwebb has sent them *two* military men. So I suggest that Boy Toby here becomes the aide to General Dzong. Two heads are better than one—and since there *might* be treachery (who knows?), whom could David trust more than his own brother?

'Now about Zillon. This is my second suggestion: when General Dzong and his aide arrive in Grunia they should announce that the downfall of Hildrok has already begun and if everyone will gather in the city square they will see the proof of that. Then, when they're all waiting, Zillon will drive in on the Wurg, to prove to all Grunia that my prophecy is coming true. I reckon that will put the whole nation solidly behind you. Well, how do you like my plan?'

All the boys agreed that Urb's ideas were sound and she then said: 'Right. Now let me see what we can do about making you into a martial figure, Toby, my lad. Hunt through the wardrobe, husband, and see how like General Dzong we can make our Captain . . . what'll we call you, Toby?'

'Well, if David's General Dzong,' said Toby promptly, 'I'll be Captain Dzing.' And so it was decided.

For the next hour David and Zillon watched the transformation of Toby into a hard-bitten warrior like General Dzong, the only difference in their appearance in the end being that Toby's false hair was black and curly, like his own, and he was wearing his glasses.

'And now,' said Urb finally, 'that's the best we can do and a more impressive pair of military mandarins I never saw in my life! So on your way and all good fortune go with you. Zillon will follow later.'

But a thought had just occurred to David. 'Take care

it's a good deal later,' he warned. 'Zillon has a fast-moving Wurg and we'll be on foot. It won't do if he passes us and arrives first in the city!'

'Come, Most Mighty General Dzong!' said Urb. 'You surely don't suppose we could let two such important people go on foot? Follow me to the yard behind the cottage. Your steeds are there and champing at the bit!'

David and Toby were relieved to hear this, for the thought of tramping for three miles on a stony road with four-inch elevators in their military boots didn't appeal to them at all.

In the yard behind the cottage a great surprise awaited them. Two large four-footed beasts stood there covered in shaggy black coats that hung down all around them almost to the ground. Towering horns like motor-cycle handlebars rose from their brows. Their saddles were of red leather, heavily tooled in gold, and their reins were thick, heavy ropes of golden silk.

'What on earth d'you call these?' exclaimed Toby, in amazement.

'You will learn as you go along,' said Urb mysteriously. 'Now mount and be on your way, for the day will soon be dying.'

So General Dzong and Captain Dzing clambered—with some difficulty—into the saddles, and at a jerk of the reins the massive animals moved off.

'Follow the track behind the trees,' called Urb. 'Thus you will pass out of sight of the Wurg, for it might be tempted to attack your animals if it is hungry. You will reach the road in a few moments and the city is but three miles from that point.

'Good luck! Good luck!' she called as they lumbered towards the trees and her husband and Zillon echoed the cry.

The day was warm, the sun was low and the shadows long and the two beasts moved along at a slow and steady pace while David and Toby talked of the things that had happened to them and speculated on what lay ahead.

In this way they had travelled some two miles when David patted his ambling steed on its shaggy rump and remarked: 'Well, Urb wouldn't tell us what they call these creatures. I wonder when we'll find out?'

And at this, from somewhere below him, a very deep

voice said: 'You're not the only one who's wearing a disguise, General Dzong! Have you forgotten riding to the rescue of Boy Toby, with three otters sitting beside you on my back? I'm Horse!'

CHAPTER 19

THE JAWS OF DEATH

DAVID and Toby were delighted to meet the horse again. 'And this,' he told them, tossing his head towards his companion, 'is the only one of us who has genuine horns on his head. You haven't met him before, Boy Toby, but I think your brother may remember him.'

Here the other animal put in, in a deep rumbling voice that seemed to come from under the earth: 'Sure, you'll remember Old Blackie, Keeper of the Door in the Council of Creatures.'

'Bull!'

'I told Horse here you wouldn't have forgotten,' answered the bull, well pleased.

The horse said: 'This is a sort of holiday for Bull. He's so full of beans that he's even been talking about racing me. Me—I ask you! As if he had a chance of winning!' and the horse let out a great whinny of laughter.

'Ho, Hauler of Wagons!' rumbled the bull. 'Look ahead. There is the southern gate of the city and I think I see the High Council drawn up to welcome our riders. How far would you say it is to the gates?'

The horse considered a moment. 'About half a mile.'

'Then let's roar down this road like an army,' said the bull, beginning to swing his great head from side to side in excitement. 'Massive show of strength and all that, to impress 'em, eh? Strike sparks with your hooves and pull up sharp under their noses in a cloud of dust. What about it?'

'You'd never keep up with me!'

'Rubbish! I'd leave you behind!'

'Think so?'

'Know so!'

'Right then! Ready . . . ?'

'Hey, hey, hey, you two!' shouted David. 'It's all right you wanting to race each other, but what are *we* supposed to do?'

'You?' answered the horse in surprise. 'Why, you just hang on, hard as you can. That's what *you* do. O.K., Bull? Then . . . *one* . . . *two* . . *three* . . . *OFF*!'

And, with a jerk that almost flung their riders off backwards the two contestants plunged down the road in a crescendo of hoof-beats that shook the country around.

The horse stretched his long neck and thrust his head forward, steam shooting from his nostrils. The bull, as bulls do, preferred to get his head down, pointing the tips of his horns straight at his objective and carrying his tail stiffly upright like a banner.

Both boys, as you can imagine, were soon in difficulties. David found himself lying flat along the horse's neck and hanging for dear life on to the false horns, which soon began to slip from side to side.

Toby, of course, had real, firmly-fixed horns to hold on to—if he could hold them *and* stay on the bull's back. But the slope down to the bull's head was so steep that he was afraid of being somersaulted on to the road ahead and pounded to pieces by those flying hooves. So, with a desperate effort, Toby managed to twist round and, grabbing the bull's tail with both hands, he lay flat along its back, peering backwards through the cloud of dust and stones that his steed threw up behind.

The only thought in Toby's mind as they came in neck and neck was: 'When, oh when, will this stop?', while David, who could see the welcoming group of High Councillors growing nearer and nearer, was asking himself: 'Can we stop in time?'

But, they did—just, though matters could have been serious if the members of the High Council hadn't leaped back about six feet through fear of being knocked down.

However, they now came forward, led by the President and Brindor the Tidings-Bearer, to greet the military mission. As befitted the leaders of a land of farmers, the members of the High Council wore sheepskin robes and on their heads long wigs of curled wood, like judges. Each Councillor carried a shepherd's crook of wood, covered in gold-leaf, as a sign of his high office.

Their appearance, as they surged round General Dzong

and Captain Dzing, with wigs askew and in some cases turned from back to front after the scare they had had, was not as impressive as it might have been. But then neither was that of their visitors, who were very much ruffled from their bumpy ride. David's big moustachios, that stuck out far on either side of his face, had slipped so much out of position that they now stood like the hands of a clock at ten minutes to four, while those of Toby were the other way round—at twenty minutes to two.

Before the throng could reach forward eager hands to help them dismount, David managed to get himself upright in the saddle. He flung up one arm and cried: 'Greetings from our leader, Captain Cobwebb, to the High Council and the People of Grunia! I am General Dzong, whom you are expecting, and Captain Cobwebb has also sent you Captain Dzing here, who is my aide. As you have just had a unique opportunity of observing, he is also a master of military horsemanship.'

'Indeed, Most Noble General and Most Intrepid Captain,' declared the President of the High Council, 'we have never seen such riding. We wonder much that Captain Dzing is able to do such a thing. Perhaps more do we wonder why he should wish to do it?'

'It is a technique he has perfected,' answered David gravely, 'whereby he can keep constant watch to make sure that enemies cannot surprise us by an attack from the rear.'

'You see, sir, what ignorant folk we are! We should never have thought of that,' exclaimed Brindor the Tidings-Bearer and David was happy to see that the father of Zillon had not recognised him as the boy he had met on the road so short a time before.

'And if we had thought of it,' commented the President drily, 'I doubt we'd have had the courage to attempt the feat. You have only to command us, General Dzong, in this matter of fighting the Wurgs. We will do whatever you say.'

Out of the corner of his eye David saw that Toby had been helped safely to the ground and had now managed to get his breath back. He noted also that dusk was falling and already, in the narrow street that led from the south gate towards the Hall of Council in the city's main square, torches were being lit in the wall sconces.

So he said, as he swung himself out of the saddle:

97

'Then I shall give my first command here and now, Mr. President. Call on all the people of the city to gather at once outside the Hall of Council. Let the Tidings-Bearer announce forthwith that they will witness this evening the fulfilment of the prophecy of Urb, the Wise Woman of Grunia. They shall see a boy, a son of this city, ride through its streets on the back of a Wurg. This wonder will herald the vanquishing of Hildrok!'

With the Councillors milling excitedly around them, David and Toby made their way to the main square while Brindor, running ahead, climbed to the Tidings Room at the top of the tower that rose above the Hall of Council. From the window of a circular room, so cunningly designed that it amplified his voice until it could be clearly heard in every street and alley of the city, he gave General Dzong's message to the citizens.

And, while the streets filled swiftly with expectant crowds, General Dzong and Captain Dzing stood, with the members of the High Council, looking towards the south gate and awaiting the arrival of Zillon.

The square was enormous and the cobblestones of its surface, polished with the traffic of generations of feet, reflected the smoky glare of the hundreds of torches that now flared from the buildings around.

There was only one patch of darkness—the gaping mouth of the great well that occupied the centre of the square. Its parapet was low and from four points around the circle curving bars of twisted iron rose up and met, holding over the centre of the hole a rusting iron pulley block; rusting because the well was now dry. The city had for years had a supply of water piped from a mountain watershed, but the Grunians were unwilling to fill in the old well and on hot days they would sit in dozens on the shallow parapet and swear that the air was always cooler there.

General Dzong and Captain Dzing stood together and gazed impassively across the mouth of the great well to the arched entrance of the southern gate.

'I hope Zillon's all right,' whispered General Dzong out of the corner of his mouth. 'I hope he gets here quickly.'

'He'll be here,' whispered Captain Dzing confidently. 'He knows how to handle that Wurg. Don't forget, I've ridden with him. Listen . . . what did I tell you?'

For at that moment a trumpet sounded from the guard at the gate and a great murmur of excitement ran through the huge, closely-packed crowds.

A moment later, to a roar of frenzied cheering, Zillon his red hair blazing like a beacon in the glare of the torches, swept into the square on the back of the huge Wurg. He rode triumphantly, one hand on the reins, the other raised high above his head as he cried 'Victory to Grunia!'

And as the cry was taken up by the multitude, until the very walls of the city seemed to tremble at the shout, Zillon gave a jerk to the reins to take the Wurg along two sides of the square and bring it to rest in front of the High Council.

But whether it was because of the shouting, or the lights, or just because at long last the Wurg had recovered from the effects of the treatment Badger had given it . . . for some reason or other, Zillon seemed suddenly unable to control it.

Then the whole crowd saw a terrible thing happen!

The Wurg, snarling with fury, began to wrestle against the pull of the reins. It champed madly on the wooden bit with its razor-sharp fangs. Suddenly with a crack, the bar of wood snapped in the middle. The two ends fell from the monster's mouth. The reins went slack and Zillon had to leap for his life. The Wurg's red eyes opened wide in blazing anger. It shook its head, swinging its heavy tentacles from side to side until they became un-knotted and streamed out stiffly behind it. Then, fixing its furious gaze on the clearest and brightest object in sight, it surged murderously forward, while screams of panic replaced the shouts of victory.

Diagonally across the square it swept, along a path that would take it directly to those two enemies that its poor sight could most easily distinguish: two military figures in uniforms of shining blue, General David Dzong and Captain Toby Dzing, who, rooted to the spot, awaited their doom.

CHAPTER 20

THE NOOSE TIGHTENS

'THIS is it!' whispered David, and together they drew their swords, determined to go down fighting.

The Wurg was nearing the further lip of the great well, coming directly at them, straight as an arrow. They tensed their muscles for the assault.

The Wurg, snarling viciously, rose slightly as it reached the broad, low parapet, and then . . . with a wild screech that echoed through the city, it vanished!

A roar of amazement went up from the cowering throng of people. David, after a moment of stupefaction, suddenly clapped Toby on the back, shouting 'Badger was right! Badger was right!'

He turned, dashed swiftly to the wall of the Hall of Council, seized a torch from its sconces and hurried Toby to the rim of the well. Down went the torch into the deep, dark shaft, twisting and turning, lighting up the smooth stone walls as it fell.

'There it is!' Toby cried.

Just for a moment the two boys had a clear view of the Wurg. Its body battered and broken, it lay in a pathetic heap on the dry bottom of the well, dead.

The High Councillors were rushing towards them now. At their head was Brindor, with an arm round the shoulders of his son Zillon. And from the shadows all around came the people of Grunia, streaming across the square. Many jabbed with their heels at the cobblestones until they could loosen them enough to grasp and pull them up: then they rained them down into the well and when David raised and waved his sword to call a halt the crowd thronged around chanting 'Long live General Dzong and Captain Dzing!'

It took David quite a long time to get a hearing and when he had done so he said:

'Listen, citizens of Grunia! Hildrok has expected the city to surrender to him without a battle. He has set tomorrow night as the limit of his patience. He will arrive outside your walls with his entire army of Wurgs. Now, you have just seen how easy it is to destroy one of these monsters. We can destroy an army of them just as easily by building a big enough pit for them to fall into. And how shall we lure them to the pit? Come close and I will tell you.'

In eager silence the huge crowd packed tight around the well-head.

'When Hildrok arrives,' said David, making his voice as deep and important-sounding as he could, 'the northern gate will be open because it is from the north he will attack. From the fields outside the city a wide avenue of triumph will lead up to the gateway and the banks of that avenue will be lit by torches, to dazzle the weak eyes of the Wurgs, and everywhere along them will wave the white flags of surrender. Make no doubt about it, Hildrok will sweep like a conqueror along that triumphal road to invest the city and wreak havoc with his Wurgs. But,—listen well!—in the darkness under the archway a deep pit will be waiting to swallow the invaders.'

David paused and Toby broke in:

'Dig the pit long and wide and very deep, with straight sides. Wurgs can climb a little, as we have found, but if the pit is deep enough they will be killed by the fall. I also suggest, with the General's permission' (and David nodded gravely), 'that you take up all the cobblestones from this square and let every citizen carry some. From the battlements above the northern gate they can wave white flags and shout "Long live Hildrok!"—and save their weightier welcome until the Wurgs are tumbling into the pit below.'

There was a roar of laughter from the crowd and a voice shouted: 'Let's start at once!' The cry was taken up all over the square.

David called for a moment's silence.

'Since this is Grunia's struggle,' he said, 'we feel that it is a Grunian citizen who should lead you to victory. Who better than he who fulfilled the prophecy of Hildrok's doom? Who better than the boy who made the Wurg his beast of burden? Who better than Zillon?'

'Zillon! Zillon!' yelled the crowd. 'Zillon for Victory!'

And Brindor of the Tidings-Bearer looked proudly on while his son took the oath of leadership.

*   *   *

General Dzong and Captain Dzing sat down with the members of the High Council to a frugal meal that night, frugal because Hildrok's constant raids on their cattle and farmsteads had made food-stocks very low. They ate to the constant noise of pick and shovel, of shouted orders and of laughter too, because now that the Grunians could see a way to end their troubles all their old fears had fallen from them.

Often David and Toby heard the name of Zillon and they soon realised that they could not have suggested a more popular leader, for Zillon, instead of merely giving orders, took up pick and shovel and dug with the rest.

In order to be within call, David and Toby had chosen as their headquarters a small court of justice on an upper floor of the Hall of Council and they went there as soon as they could to talk over the events of the day and to get some rest.

'Well, Badger was way ahead of us in finding the weakness of the Wurgs,' said David happily. ' "*When it stops, they drops*" he said. They can hold themselves a few inches above the ground and even when there's a slope they can keep the same distance above it. But if they suddenly find themselves over a hole then they have to drop to the bottom. They might get only a heavy jolt if it was a shallow hole; but dig a deep enough pit and they're done for. Hildrok knows it because he must have constructed that huge ramp that leads down into the Pit of Wurgs. What Hildrok will find out too late is that his secret has been discovered. Good old Badger!'

'Hear, hear!' agreed Toby. 'Now let's get some sleep.'

Their camp-beds were placed side by side in the well of the court and as they looked up from their pillows there loomed over them the raised platform and the judge's vast oak chair over which Wisdom and Justice were represented by an owl holding a pair of scales.

'I like that,' David commented. 'I think it's much more sensible to have a wise old owl holding the scales than a blindfold woman like we have in our country.'

Toby looked up for a moment.

'I think they could have done better than that, though,' he said critically. 'They could at least have had a carving, in wood or something, instead of a stuffed owl—badly stuffed at that, and moth-eaten by the look of it.' And he gave the surprised David a big wink.

Down came the scales with a crash on to the judge's desk. And down from his perch came Owl and began to pace up and down between the two beds, hoisting each shoulder in turn and fluffing out his wings.

'Badly-stuffed! Moth-eaten!' he said. 'Good job I saw you wink, Boy Toby, or I'd have nipped your ears off. You should have seen the monstrosity they had up there! I pitched it out of the window. Anyhow, congratulations on spotting me. Your eyesight must be improving. I gather things went well for you today,' went on the owl. 'And that's why Captain Cobwebb sent me to ask you a question. Here it is: do you think you could get away from here tomorrow afternoon? Will the Grunians be able now to manage on their own?'

The two boys nodded.

'Sure of it,' said David.

'Absolutely certain,' Toby agreed.

'That's good, then,' said the owl. 'The idea is for the two of you to get back to the top of the mountain over Hildrok's fortress and seal the whole place up so that no Wurgs can ever get above ground by that route again. And also,' added the owl, waving one claw warningly, 'so that no-one can ever get back *into* the place again. We hope Hildrok himself won't escape your trap, but if he should do so then we want him kept out in the open where he can be hunted down.'

'That makes sense,' said David, slowly. 'And I'm sure Horse and Bull, who are eating their heads off in the stable here, will get us there on time.'

'Provided they don't start racing and chuck us off,' said Toby, feelingly.

'Don't worry about that,' answered the owl. 'It's a long way, and all uphill. And they know it.'

'All right,' said David. 'Let's suppose all goes well and we get there. You say casually *"seal the place up"*, Owl. How are we supposed to do that?'

'Simple,' said the owl. 'As Boy Toby knows already, there's a pool that provides the water to work all the doors in Hildrok's fortress. To block all the doors all you have to do is to empty the pool.'

'Wait a minute! Wait a minute!' Toby protested. 'You're the one who told me that it couldn't be done. *"Take ages to empty"*, you said, *"even if you had a pipe . . . even if there was no rain"*. Now you tell us it'll be easy. What's made you change your mind? How are we supposed to do this job?'

'I don't know,' replied the owl, irritably. 'You'll find out when you get there.'

'That's no answer!' Toby objected.

'Well, it's the only one I can give you,' snapped the owl. '*He* said he'd found out exactly how it could be done and it was so easy you'd be surprised you'd never thought of it. So I said *"Tell me"* because I wanted to be able to tell *you*. But he couldn't.'

'Why ever not?'

'Because he'd forgotten. But he'll have remembered by the time you get there. I hope.'

'Look here,' said David, light beginning to dawn, 'who is this "he"?'

'You know,' said the owl, '. . . Old Worryguts . . . Old Mumble-mumble . . .'

'Old Daddy Badger!'

'Of course,' answered the owl. 'Now stop arguing and tell me: will you go?'

'Of course,' said David.

'Badger hasn't failed us yet,' added Toby.

At this the owl put his head down and drew his shoulders up so high that they almost covered it.

'Badger, Badger, Badger!' he hooted, grumblingly. 'It's always Badger. He's the Clever One, he is. He's the Bright Boy. Oh, there's nobody but Badger. Nobody else gets noticed, for all they may do.'

'Don't you believe it, Owl,' said Toby stoutly. 'What would have been the use of all Badger's cleverness if you hadn't got me and Zillon out of Hildrok's clutches?'

'None at all,' declared David, with a wink at Toby that the owl didn't notice this time.

'So you see, Owl,' Toby added, 'although you hate so much to admit it, you are really very wonderful.'

The owl's head came up sharply and his big round eyes swung from side to side like a lighthouse beacon.

'Oh, I've no objection to admitting I'm wonderful,' he said. 'It's just that I don't like having to raise the matter myself. But as you've mentioned it, yes, I do realise that I'm a pretty wonderful creature. Quite wonderful, in fact. Right, then,' went on the owl in a business-like tone. 'So we see you tomorrow up at the pool?'

'Yes,' said David.

'And even if Badger forgets his great idea for emptying it,' Toby added, 'we're quite confident that you'll be ready with a much better one.'

'Of course. Who could doubt it?' answered the owl as he vanished silently through the skylight.

CHAPTER 21

BADGER KEEPS THEM GUESSING

ALL that night and past noon of the following day the work of preparing the Grunian trap for Hildrok's army went on. Inspired by Zillon's example, everybody, from the smallest toddler who could carry a cobblestone, right up to the President of the High Council, lent a hand. General Dzong and Captain Dzing walked around inspecting the work and graciously acknowledging the greetings they received on every hand.

Captain Dzing was much impressed by their reception.

'You know, David,' he said to General Dzong, 'you used to say you wanted to join the army and *I* used to say I never would. But I'm not so sure now. I think I'll come in with you, provided we can both start at the top like this and be Generals. It's easy work.'

'It's not *that* easy being a General,' protested David.

' 'Course it is. Look around. We get all the cheers and none of the chores!'

'Oh, you are daft! Anyway, it'd be ages before you could be a General. You have to start at the bottom —squarebashing and peeling potatoes and working in the cookhouse.'

'They have cooks in an army? Real cooks?'

'Of course they do, you idiot!'

'But there has to be somebody in charge of the cooks? Somebody who knows how to cook, I mean, not just an ordinary General?'

'Yes, yes, yes!'

'Then that settles it,' declared Captain Toby Dzing. 'You join the army and be General. And I'll come in with you as Cook General. That's even more important than just being a General, you know, because they say an army marches on its stomach.'

'If you don't shut up,' answered General Dzong wrathfully, 'I'll *jump* on yours!'

Fortunately that possibility was averted by the arrival of Zillon who came to invite them to inspect the finished work at the northern gate of the city.

Right under the gateway itself the Grunians had dug the biggest, deepest pit and with the smoothest, straightest sides that could be imagined. The last ladders, length after length lashed together, were drawn up as David and Toby arrived.

The fantastic amount of earth that had been dug out had been made into enormous high walls enclosing the triumphal way that stretched out from the gate for half a mile. Long torches, ready to light, were placed along each wall, interspersed with tall poles from which fluttered white flags of surrender.

'You'll notice,' said Zillon, 'that there are no torches near the gate on either side, so there'll be no chance of anyone spotting the edge of the pit.'

'How about your ammunition?'

'The cobblestones? They're piled in banks all round the square, ready for use. But you should see the battlements! Everyone who's waving a welcome flag for Hildrok will have a pile of stones beside him. To drive the message home,' laughed Zillon.

David and Toby complimented Grunia's leader on his preparations and then David raised the question of their departure to try to seal up Hildrok's fortress while he was riding to attack the city.

'Don't worry,' said Zillon. 'You have set our feet on the right track and we are confident of success. Also, sealing up Hildrok's bolt-hole is a sound idea and it should be carried out.'

'We want to get away quietly, and as soon as possible,' David told him. 'We'll be glad to get out of these stuffy uniforms, especially these boots! And I'm sure the horse and the bull will travel more easily if we take off their disguises, too. We'll slip out through the southern gate. We can't afford the time to stop and return all the stuff to Urb. Could you get it back to her, sometime, with our thanks?'

'I'll see it is returned,' said Zillon. 'But if you want to thank Urb—well, come and meet her!'

They found the Wise Woman and her sturdy husband seated on a broad bench on the battlements, right over the pit beneath the northern gate, and surrounded by piles of cobblestones.

'Wouldn't miss this for anything, me boys!' chuckled Urb, weighing a cobblestone in each hand. 'I'm a bit weary of making prophecies and having to wait a long time for the results. This time I'm going to make instant prophecies and have instant results. *"Hey, Wurg, I prophesy you're going to have a big surprise"* . . . and *"Bonk! Here it is!"* '

David and Toby thanked Urb for her help and told her of their next task. Urb pursed her lips.

'I know that pool,' she said. 'Went there some years ago. But how you can possibly empty it and *keep it empty* I just can't see. Badger says it can be done? Then it *can* be done. And if Badger's forgotten the answer you can be sure that he'll remember it. But *when* he'll remember it —that's the problem. Might take months! And he won't be hurried. Don't forget that!'

*   *   *

An hour later two boys in jeans, one riding a cart-horse and the other a plodding old bull, slipped out of the southern gate, unnoticed by anyone, and set off for the pool on the mountain-top.

The horse, who knew the country well, took them by a long roundabout route that linked up with a mountain track much less steep than the way Toby and Zillon had come down on their way to Urb's cottage. All the same it was quite steep enough for even the horse to admit that it was becoming hard going, so David and Toby jumped down and went beside their friends on foot.

'I notice nobody's talking about racing this time,' puffed the horse.

'Hrrrmph!' said the bull, and left it at that.

Night had fallen by the time they reached the top, came out of the forest and began the gentle slope down to the pool. A waning moon shone from a cloudless sky and it was very cold.

'I don't know about piping the water out of here,'

commented the bull as he pushed his muzzle into the pool and sent sparkling ripples scurrying across the surface. 'Right now I feel I could drink it dry.'

'Hear, hear,' the horse agreed.

The owl dropped silently from nowhere, like a feather.

'Hildrok will be leaving any minute now,' he said, 'and if we're going to do anything useful about this pool we'll have to get busy as soon as he's out of the way. Where's that bumbling old ditherer, Badger?'

'Haven't seen him. Wasn't here when we arrived,' said the horse.

'Then we're going to have trouble with him,' said the owl crossly. 'I told him to be sure to meet you at the point where the track comes out of the forest, that being a more comfortable spot to wait in than down here on the cold rock. I was a fool,' declared the owl. 'I was mad. Because, of course, what has happened is that dopey old Badger has wandered round until he's found a nice hole or a pile of leaves and he's gone to sleep.'

'Then let's get busy and look for him,' said the horse, making a move towards the forest.

'That's only the first difficulty,' grumbled the owl as they all trekked back up the slope. 'Because when we find him—if we do find him—it'll take him so long to gather his sleepy wits together that Hildrok can be back here and tucked away inside his fortress in safety before we learn how to empty this pool.'

'Always provided,' remarked the bull, heavily, 'that Badger can remember how he'd decided it should be done.'

With such gloomy thoughts in their minds the five of them decided to space themselves out in a very large circle under the trees and then work slowly towards the centre, calling Badger's name as they did so.

It was no use. They all came together in a small clearing, with never a trace of Badger.

'We could go on like this all night long,' said the owl disgustedly.

'I could kick that Badger!' declared the horse, and to ease his feelings he lashed out with his big hooves against a log and sent it crashing into a tree.

'And I only wish he was inside it!' said the owl.

'Aarr, do 'ee then? Well, he were,' said a deep, slow

108

voice, and the badger came lumbering slowly towards them. 'He were inside and having a quiet nap. To which every animal is entitled,' declared the badger, 'without folk butting in and disturbing him. I always says . . .' he was going on when the owl cut him short.

'You were supposed to be waiting by the track there to meet Boy David and Boy Toby when they arrived,' he snapped.

'Anyway, it's all right now that we've found you,' said David soothingly. 'You were going to tell us, Badger, how we could empty this pool and see that it stayed empty. Owl says you discovered how to do it but then it slipped your mind. It's very important, Badger. Can you remember now?'

'To get rid of water in pool,' mumbled the badger, 'mm . . . mm . . . yes. to empty the pool . . . arr, yes! I got it now! The answer is simple: *when it stops, they drops*. That's it all right.'

At this there was pandemonium. Owl screeched, Horse neighed, Bull roared. And David clenched his fists and beat his forehead.

Badger waited until the row died down. ' 'Twas a simple thing, really,' he said modestly, 'and not worth all that applause.'

Owl looked as if he were about to explode, but Toby checked him with a gesture. He'd just had an idea.

'You worked that out very well, Badger,' he said, while the others looked at him in amazement. 'We had another problem as well and you solved that for us. But we forget what you told us.'

'Aarr?' said the badger.

'We wanted to know how we could beat the Wurgs,' said Toby, patiently. 'And you told us how to set about it. Now just what was it we had to do?'

'Beating Wurgs . . . yes, I did tell 'ee what to do,' said the badger. 'Why, yes I distinctly remember. I said to you, I said, *fill her up and she'll empty*. That was it.'

There was a moment's stupefied silence.

And then Toby had seized David's hands and was waltzing him round and round and shouting at the top of his voice. 'Of course! Of course! Good old Badger! That's the way to do it!'

As he paused for breath, they all heard from far below a strident trumpet call. And under the white moonlight the silvery hordes of Hildrok's murderous Wurgs surged across the fields to the waiting city of Grunia.

CHAPTER 22

THE TWILIGHT OF HILDROK

THE owl said: 'Perhaps you'll be so good as to explain, Boy Toby, how anybody can empty a pool by filling it?'

'You fill it with rocks and stones or earth,' answered Toby, 'and that pushes the water out. Simple!'

'So simple we never thought of it,' said David.

'I wish I could understand what goes on in that queer head of Badger's,' said the horse, 'and how he can be so muddled and always so right in the end.'

'I think Badger likes problems, you know,' suggested Toby. 'He works them out slowly step by step and, by the time he's got the answer, the original question doesn't interest him any longer and he forgets it. So when you raise a subject with him again he's likely to give you the right answer to the wrong problem, if you understand me.'

'We understand you,' said the owl, sourly. 'And we quite realise that Badger's wonderful. But when it comes to doing the job, then that's a matter for somebody else while he goes to sleep again. Look at him!'

And indeed the owl was quite right, for the badger had curled up into a big furry ball and was fast asleep and snoring gently.

'I reckon this is a job for the heavy mob,' remarked the horse. 'Come on, Bull, let's show 'em how fast we can move rocks.'

The bull was looking rather disgusted at the owl's display of jealousy. 'Sure,' he said, 'let's get going. Come on, Owl. Which rocks are *you* going to shift?'

The owl ducked his head, pulled his shoulders up over his ears and tramped to and fro with his sailor's rolling walk, muttering under his breath.

Already the horse and the bull had set the great boul-

110

ders rolling into the water, the bull by hooking his horns under them and simply heaving them in, and the horse with terrific double punches from his enormously strong hind-legs.

David gave Toby a nudge and they started whispering together, but not so low that the owl could not hear.

'What rudeness!'

'And to a wonderful bird like Owl!'

'We need his help so much.'

'But you can't expect him to give it now.'

'No. That's the trouble. We all have to suffer for Bull's bad temper.'

'Yes. Alas,' (said Toby, with a heartrending sigh), 'I fear we shall fail without Owl's help.'

All this time he had been watching the owl out of the corner of his eye and seen him edge closer and closer.

Now the owl gave a little cough. 'Ahem,' he said. 'Is anything the matter? You seem to be troubled.'

'We are indeed, Owl,' said Toby. 'You see, the difference between success and failure in this task depends on you. We were relying on you.'

'But with Bull having offended you so much . . .' said David.

'We didn't dare to ask . . .' added Toby.

The owl fluffed out his chest. 'Oh, dare away, dare away,' he said. 'I shall be only too glad to help *you*. *You* understand me. *You* know that brains are far more important than brawn. What's the problem?'

Toby said: 'You see, Owl, we need to know just how the battle for Grunia is going, and only you can tell us that. Horse and Bull may think that they have all night to fill up that pool. But suppose, for instant, that Hildrok has discovered the trap that the Grunians have set. He may simply turn round, dash back here and arrive before Horse and Bull have finished the job. But with you watching from the sky and letting us know what was happening, we could speed up the work and beat Hildrok to it.'

'Our Spy in the Sky!' declared David, impressively. 'Who but Owl could do such a job?'

'Will you undertake this Secret Mission, Owl?' begged Toby.

The owl spread and flexed his wings.

'Where Duty calls, Owl will be there,' he said. 'Rely on me.' And he vanished silently into the sky.

The boys went over to help the bull and horse, whose work had already made a great difference, for as the bed of the pool began to fill with rocks, the water overflowed and was now spreading towards the lip of the sheer rock-face in which was the huge door of Hildrok's fortress.

They must have been at work for about an hour when, suddenly, there was the owl, strutting towards them. He passed the horse and bull with his beak in the air and halted before David.

'Here is Spy in the Sky, reporting from Secret Mission,' he declared portentously.

'Welcome, Pie in the Sky,' said the horse, with a raucous horse-laugh. But the owl was far too full of his own importance even to hear him.

'First Report,' said Owl. 'Arrived over destination 0340 hours. Observations: triumphal way to northern gate of Grunia illuminated by torches. White flags waving. Battlements crowded with citizens waving flags and shouting: "Long live Hildrok". Approaching triumphal way from surrounding fields, great shoal of Wurgs. Estimated number six hundred. Heard Hildrok urging them on with cries of "*Into the city square. Then spread out and kill . . . kill . . . kill!*' Then, with Hildrok bringing up the rear, Wurgs proceeded at great speed towards city gate.'

Owl paused and cleared his throat.

'Well come on, Pie in the Sky,' said the horse impatiently. 'Tell us what happened.'

'What're we supposed to do now?' rumbled the bull. 'Wait for next week's thrilling instalment?'

'Military reports have to be given in chronological order,' said the owl coldly. Then he went on:

'Second Report. Attempted entry of city by Hildrok's forces . . . Oh!' cried the owl suddenly, hopping from one foot to the other and forgetting all his reserve, '. . . you should have seen it! The Wurgs went dashing along down the road between those high banks, dazzled by all the torches and, if any of them did see the pit ahead of them it came too late because of the great pressure from the Wurgs behind, and down they went—down into the blackness! The cobblestones fell like hail. And everybody was shouting now "Down with Hildrok"! And then Hildrok,

112

astride those two great battle-Wurgs of his, came roaring up to the pit edge . . .' The owl stopped to draw breath.

'Go on, go on!' neighed the horse.

'Just as they got there he saw the trap. The Wurgs dropped into the pit like stones but Hildrok let go the reins and he jumped. A fantastic leap! He got his hands on the lowest rail of the portcullis, right in the point of the archway. Then he swung himself—like a man shooting off a trapeze—he flung himself right through the arch, right over the pit, and landed in the city square.'

'And he was killed at once by the people,' said the bull, anticipating.

'He wasn't,' answered the owl. 'Some came forward to attack him but most held back. The ones that Hildrok could reach he picked up in bunches in those great steel talons of his. Some he flung into the pit among his dying Wurgs and some he dashed against the city walls. Then Urb, the Wise Woman, took a hand. She was up in the battlements, over the city gate. She leaned over and she shouted: *"Hildrok, Hildrok! Look at me and hear my prophecy!"* He caught the words. He halted and looked towards her. *"Hard times are ahead for you,"* cried Urb —hitting him between the eyes with a cobblestone.

'And that was *that*,' ended David.

'No!' spluttered the owl. 'He went down. The people surged forward to stone him to death. But Hildrok staggered to his feet. He ran at them and as he went forward they gave way before him. Then they closed in from behind and the stoning began. They drove him up against the city wall and thought they had him cornered. But he dug his claws into the wall, clambered to the battlements, flung the defenders there right and left, climbed down the other side. He went staggering across the meadows in this direction and vanished into a clump of trees. I estimate,' ended the owl, panting, 'that he'll be here in about two hours. End of report. Spy in the Sky signing off.'

'Well!' commented the bull admiringly. 'That was as good as having a front seat at the show. I hand it to you, Owl, I really do. You're a wonderful old bird.'

'I knew you'd find that out eventually,' answered the owl.

*　　　*　　　*

The owl's estimate was correct. The bed of the pool was almost full of rocks and the channels that supplied water to work the doors were becoming blocked with rubble. The displaced flood was rippling ever nearer the brink of the cliff face when they saw, far below, the tiny figure of Hildrok weaving drunkenly towards his fortress.

'Hurry, hurry, Bull!' hooted the owl, on tenterhooks. 'Hurry—or he'll beat you to it!'

'Take it easy, Owl,' answered the bull, 'and keep out of the way. This is where we unveil our secret weapon.'

The bull and the horse clattered over to a gigantic boulder that projected from a steep section of the slope above the pool.

'We've loosened this already,' said the horse. 'One good heave—and down it'll come, along with the tons and tons of earth that it's holding in place. We're ready, Owl, as soon as you give us the signal.'

Hildrok reached the rock face. He stamped a foot, to work the mechanism of the fortress door. With a loud grinding sound the huge barrier rose an inch or so, faltered, then fell back. Hildrok looked up in dismay, realising that something was wrong with the water supply that worked the door. He flung himself against the cliff face, all claws outstretched, and began to climb.

The owl gave a low hoot and raised one large white wing.

'*NOW*!' roared the bull. He hooked his horns round one end of the boulder and levered away, while, at the other end, the horse put every ounce of his weight and muscle into a mighty double punch from his hind legs.

The enormous boulder tilted, tottered, and fell. Behind it a vast avalanche of earth and stones came thundering down to force every vestige of water from the bed of the pool. The flood swept over the cliff edge like a Niagara, smashing Hildrok to the ground.

Lying flat on the rock, peering over the edge, David and Toby saw him, battered but still unbeaten, begin to struggle to his feet.

And at that moment they heard dimly, from far below, a cry of '*Up, lads and at 'em*!' and three lithe black figures sprang from the shadows into the moonlight and flung themselves snarling and snapping at the fugitive.

'The otters!' cried David.

114

Hildrok stumbled to his feet. He turned. He began to run. As he did so, from the blackness of the woodlands all around there broke out a bloodcurdling cacophony of howling, barking, squawking and screeching.

'What on earth's that?' demanded Toby.

'The creatures are at the heels of Hildrok,' said the owl, solemnly. 'From now on they will allow him no rest by day or night. They are herding him along the way they wish him to take, out into the Wasteland and into a trap from which there is no escape. Are you ready to follow him?'

'Us? What do you mean, Owl?' asked David.

'Hildrok is of human shape,' answered the owl, 'and Captain Cobwebb has said that the creatures may trap him. But it will be for you, being also human, to capture him or face him in battle. Are you prepared to undertake that task?

'Because if you are,' said the owl, 'then let's be on our way.'

CHAPTER 23

THE TRAP CLOSES

'WELL, Toby,' said David. 'What d'you think about that?'

'The point is,' said Toby, 'that so long as Hildrok is at large all the creatures will be in danger because there'll always be the chance that he'll turn up again with another lot of Wurgs. The Wurgs don't just kill other creatures for food: they kill them for the sake of killing, and that's against all animal law. I reckon it's up to us to go after him.'

'Then that's settled, Owl,' said David. 'We're ready.'

The horse and the bull had come up while the owl was talking.

'I take it we're in this, too, Owl?' said the horse.

'Of course.'

'Right. Now, you boys,' said the horse, 'if you're likely to end up this chase doing battle with a horror like Hildrok, you need as much rest as you can get. So I suggest we do three hours on and two hours off. Agree?'

Both David and Toby looked puzzled at this remark.

The bull explained: 'What Horse means is that you ride on our backs for three hours, then we all rest, sleep, or eat during the next two. And so on. At that rate we should pretty soon be in sight of Hildrok and when we catch him up he'll be tired and weary and you'll be fit and fresh.'

'That's a very sound idea, Bull,' said David.

'There's only one snag,' Toby put in. 'What about food?'

'We can discuss that matter just as well on the move as standing here,' said the owl, irritably.

So they mounted their steeds, and set off as the sun rose, with the owl perched on one of the bull's horns.

'Such a pity you don't eat grass,' said the horse.

'Grass builds muscle, you know,' commented the bull to Toby.

'Ugh!' said Toby. 'What I want is bee-'

'Beans!' interjected David loudly. 'What he likes is beans . . . and peas . . . and potatoes . . . and things.' And he whispered fiercely to Toby: '*You don't talk to a bull about liking beefsteak!*'

'H'm. No beans around these parts,' said the owl. 'I don't suppose you'd care to share a few field-mice with me? No?' (he saw the look on Toby's face). 'I have it! Nuts, berries, fruit—you'll eat those? Right, then I'll pass the word around and we'll have some collected in the woods and sent out to us every day.'

'Out?'

'Out into the Wasteland—where we'll be. Look, Horse, you tell 'em about it while I go and make arrangements about their food.' And the owl flew off silently.

'If you look ahead,' said the horse, 'you'll see that after we've crossed this valley we go uphill again through a forest. Just at the top of that far hill a sort of road begins. It grows wider and wider until it is about a mile across, and the forest forms a kind of hedge on each side. That piece in the middle we call the Wasteland because nothing grows on it.

'The forest runs at each side of the Wasteland for many miles. Then suddenly, between each wall of the forest and the Wasteland, there opens a deep canyon and the

Wasteland goes on for a day's march until it reaches the place we call the Edge of the World.'

'Why's that?' asked David.

'Because there the land ends,' said the horse, solemnly. 'Beyond it there is nothing—nothing but space and clouds.'

'And that's where Hildrok is being driven,' said the bull. 'Because when he gets there he is trapped. He can run no further. He must surrender or fight to the death.'

'He won't surrender,' said David. 'We'll have to fight him.'

They ambled on, Toby with his head down and muttering a great deal under his breath. David edged the horse a little nearer and leaned over towards his brother to try to catch his words.

'And when we've beaten Hildrok,' (Toby was muttering) 'then everybody will be praising us and they'll all come round and they'll say *"How did you beat Hildrok, David and Toby? To what do you owe your success?"* And we'll say *"We owe it to the strength of our stout right arms."* And then they'll say: *"And to what do you owe the strength of your stout right arms?"* Well, David can say what he likes—but I'm not going to say: *"I owe the strength of my stout right arm to nuts, berries and fruit."* So there!'

*　　*　　*

The day passed without sign of the owl but when the first rest period of the evening came along he was back, and following soon afterwards came three old friends, bearing sacks of food for the two boys.

'Hiya!' Otter Number One greeted them. 'Anything you want, mates, always ask the otters. Here y'are—loverly grub. Courtesy of the Otter Catering Service.'

And Number Two, as he saw Toby reaching for a luscious red fruit, something like a large apple, giggled: 'You'll love every bite. Every mouthful has our own distinctive fish-oil flavour.'

Toby dropped the fruit as if it were red-hot but the eldest otter, Number Three, clipped the giggler over one ear with a paw. 'Take no notice of him,' he said. 'I made him wash his paws before I'd even let him carry the bag.'

'What's the news of Hildrok, Otters?' asked the owl.

'Well, as you know,' said Number Three, 'we defeated his army at Grunia and chased him from the field of battle . . .'

'Here, that's not what I saw!' exclaimed the owl.

'And where was you at the time, mate?' asked Number One.

'Him?' giggled Number Two. 'I'll tell you where Owl was . . . *Up above the Wurgs so high, Sitting safely in the sky* . . . Weren't you, Owl?'

'That'll do, now!' said Number One, sharply. 'Owl's a good friend of ours and I won't have him made fun of. Old he may be. A bit short-sighted and somewhat forgetful. But in his day—in his day, mark you—Owl was a force to be reckoned with.'

The sheer cheek of this quite took the owl's breath away and before he could recover, the otter went on:

'Yes, as usual, it was victory for the otters. Hildrok fled back to his fortress. But the otters had been there first and jammed the door so he couldn't get in.'

'We chased him off,' cried Number One.

'We herded him like a sheep,' giggled Number Two.

'And now we're keeping him running into the Wasteland,' said Number Three. 'We get him into the trap and leave the rest to you.'

'Nothing to worry about now,' said Number One.

'Push him over the Edge of the World—and that's the end of him,' chanted the giggler.

'So go right ahead, with confidence,' said Number Three. 'We've done the hard work for you.'

The owl could bottle up his feelings no longer.

'I have never heard such a farrago of nonsense!' he exploded. 'Upon my word, you otters are the greatest, the most arrant perverters of the truth I . . . I . . . I . . .'

Number Three interrupted him with a squeal of delight.

'Hey, listen to that, boys! Even Owl admits that the otters are the greatest . . . the greatest . . . whatever-it-is, but anyway the greatest!'

The owl's screech of rage was drowned by a great roar, and the bull came charging, horns down, at his friend's tormentors.

But you don't catch an otter napping.

*　　　*　　　*

When the otters became too swanky, the Bull would lose his temper and charge them. (Only 2p each as they didn't have much pocket money.)

The chase after Hildrok went on day after weary day. The hawk and the owl kept alternate watch and reported on the fugitive's position. The animals were managing to confine his route to the wild country of the Wasteland. Every time he made an effort to seek shade and shelter in the forest, he was met by the bared fangs and unsheathed claws of hundreds upon hundreds of creatures.

Despite Hildrok's injuries, however, his strength semed for a while to be sufficient to bear him on for many miles. But at length he began to flag. At the end of a week he was staggering from side to side. A week later and he would often fall to the ground and lie there for a time before he could recover the strength to rise.

There came one day when Hildrok turned and saw the figures of David and Toby in the distance. His keen eyes told him who they were. He raised his arm high and shook his fist at them. Anger seemed to restore his strength and he plunged forward again, hoping that somewhere, soon, the Wasteland must give way to lush pastures where there were cattle he could slaughter to satisfy his gargantuan appetite, or where there were woods and hills and hiding places that would give him shelter until he had recovered his forces.

But now the pursuers were nearing the point where the Wasteland became an unfenced track between two deep canyons.

And as they did so, David and Toby noticed a curious change in the attitude of the animals.

The otters ceased to be gay and brash and appeared fearful and unhappy. The day that Hildrok first set foot upon the track between the canyons the forests seemed to have become empty of creatures. A strange silence brooded by day and by night.

One evening the otters deposited the bag of food for David and Toby, mumbled something about not coming back, and slouched away, heads hanging.

The hawk vanished from the sky without a further visit to them to report on Hildrok's progress. This did not matter very much because by now they had him in sight. But the horse and the bull were becoming very moody and the owl would often sit on the bull's horn for an hour at a time and mope without saying a word.

At last, one morning, the horse stopped.

'Get down, boys, please,' he said. 'We've all been afraid to tell you, but now we've simply got to speak.'

He looked round at the others. The bull slowly nodded his big head. The owl ruffled his feathers, hunched his shoulders over his head and looked most unhappy.

'Boy David. Boy Toby,' said the horse, slowly. 'We thought we'd be able to go on. We thought we'd be able to bear it. But we've realised that we can't. None of us can. *No* animal can. We've got to turn back, boys. From here you'll have to go on to that last meeting with Hildrok alone.'

CHAPTER 24

WHAT HAPPENED TO HILDROK

'But I don't understand, Horse,' said David. 'What is it that you can't bear?'

'He means the killing, Boy David,' put in the bull. 'You know that Hildrok will not give himself up. How can he, when he knows that he would be put in prison? To be caged is worse than death, as every animal knows. So he will fight and you will have to kill him or be killed.'

'That's the risk we take in trying to see that justice is done,' said Toby. 'Can't you understand that?'

'I'm afraid we can't,' said the owl. 'Animals kill to eat, to survive. That's the only law we understand. It would upset us greatly to see killing being done for any other reason. Because once you admit that there can be any other reason, where's the killing going to end?'

'There's also this point,' said the horse. 'We can't bring ourselves to see this final battle because to us animals Hildrok and you are all humankind. We've always hoped that one day men would stop killing us for what they call "sport". Is that ever likely to happen when men are so ready even to kill each other?'

'Please do try to see our point of view,' said the owl.

'You must follow your own law,' David answered, 'and we must obey ours. So let us say good-bye here and we will go on alone to meet Hildrok.'

'Goodbye, Owl,' said Toby. 'And Horse. And Bull. We think you're *all* wonderful!'

And as the animals turned their backs and went slowly away, the two boys marched resolutely in the steps of Hildrok towards the Edge of the World.

They plunged ahead, determined to come up with him and settle the matter as quickly as possible. On either side of the Wasteland the canyons became wider and still wider, black and bottomless. Then the land on each side, beyond the canyons, began to fall back and the Wasteland track stretched out, far, far ahead like a vast pier, with nothing but black emptiness below it and around, while above there was only a cloudless blue sky that faded gradually into the darkness of the depths below.

Soon they could see the end of the track, and near to it on the ground the massive figure of Hildrok. They hurried forward and were almost upon him when his eyes opened. In one bound he was on his feet, stretched to his full height, towering over them with his great claws resting on his hips.

'And now, young kinsfolk of Captain Cobwebb,' growled Hildrok, 'what do you propose to do?'

'To take you back with us to be judged for your crimes,' said David stoutly.

And Toby added: 'For sending your murderous Wurgs against innocent animals and against the peaceful people of Grunia, who never did you any harm.'

'Oho!' cried Hildrok. 'How do *you* know what the peaceful people of Grunia did or did not do to me?'

'They've told us,' said David. 'You were found, helpless and abandoned, in some animal's lair. You were taken to Grunia, where a farmer gave you shelter and cared for you and gave you work. You repaid him by destroying his cattle and finally you slaughtered him and his family.'

'And for this you think it right that I should be punished?'

'Of course,' declared Toby, firmly.

'And so I should,' answered Hildrok, 'if that story were true. Let me tell you what *I* remember. I was found by a woodman who sold me to a farmer for a few pence. The farmer saw a way of making money out of me by showing me as a freak. He housed me in a sty among his pigs and his visitors paid to see my antics when he prodded me to make me bare my teeth, unsheathe my talons, or squeal with anger. But folk grew weary of coming to see the strange man-animal and no more money fell into the farmer's pocket. For this he blamed me. He beat me and he starved me and made me a beast of burden about the farm.

'One night I was so hungry that I killed one of his cattle and devoured it. For this he and his family bound me to a post set in a pile of faggots. They said they would roast me. But I was stronger now and as one of them came up with a torch to start the flames around my feet, I broke loose. They ran in terror into the house and barred the door, but the torch they left behind. I picked it up and hurled it through a window. They were the ones who were burned to death, not me. The rest, how the towns-people ran me down and sealed me in the rocks, you know.'

There was a long and very embarrassed silence.

'We didn't know that side of the story,' said David slowly.

'We never thought to ask you,' said Toby, in a very small voice.

'But,' said Hildrok wearily, 'you did not hesitate to judge me, although you knew only one side of the story.'

'We're sorry for that,' said David.

'Both of us. Very sorry, Hildrok,' added Toby.

'Those are kinder words than I have ever had yet from any human,' said Hildrok. 'But do you still intend to take me prisoner—if you can?'

'We must, Hildrok,' said Toby. 'You broke the law so you'll have to go to trial.'

'But you can be sure that both sides of the case will be put before the court,' David urged. 'Believe me, you'll get a fair hearing.'

'How can I believe you?' asked Hildrok. 'I have not harmed you. I have no quarrel with you. Leave me and go away. I will not come before your court.'

'Then we'll have to try to make you come,' said David. Toby stood close beside him. They were determined, but terribly afraid.

'You are prepared to fight *me*?'

The two boys nodded. They could not speak.

'You are brave,' said Hildrok, and added with a laugh, 'and very foolhardy to say such words when you are so

123

close to me. From where I stand I could seize you in my claws before you could draw those knives I see in your belts. But I will not take an unfair advantage. See, I turn my back on you. Turn your backs on me and we will each walk ten paces. Then we turn—and it will be death for you or for me! *One . . . two . . . three . . .*'

David and Toby paced along side by side, with their hands on the hilts of their knives.

'*Four . . . five . . . six . . .*' came Hildrok's firm tones.

'Here it comes, Toby,' whispered David.

'I'll do my best,' whispered Toby, unsteadily.

'*Seven . . . eight . . .*'

'And now *nine*,' said David softly.

'*Nine . . . ten*,' Hildrok called.

David and Toby swung round to face the attack.

But no attack came. Twenty paces away Hildrok stood facing them, standing on the very Edge of the World.

'You see I have tricked you,' he said, laughing. 'You cannot reach me in time to stop me doing what I have decided to do. I will not come with you. But I cannot bring myself to kill you. Goodbye and good fortune go with you!'

And with that he stepped calmly to his death over the Edge of the World and into the black emptiness of boundless Space.

CHAPTER 25

MR. GREEN TELLS A FISHY STORY

DAVID and Toby turned and hurried as fast as they could to get away from that awful spot. Night was falling when at last they reached the place where the two canyons ended and the forest once again fenced in the Wasteland.

They flung themselves down on the warm sandy soil to rest, and neither of them spoke for a long time.

Then David said: 'I can't help feeling sorry for Hildrok.'

'Me too,' said Toby.

And then nothing more was said for quite a while until

Toby asked: 'David, what do you think's happening in Grunia now?'

'I don't know.'

'Well, couldn't we find out?'

'How d'you mean, "find out". What d'you expect me to do, look for a telephone?'

'There may be no telephones, but what about your transistor set? Is that all right?'

'Seems all right,' said David, pulling the set out of his pocket.

'Well, we were able to listen-in to people talking in Grunia once before,' Toby pointed out. 'Why not try again?'

So David switched on the set and he twiddled the knob this way and that, but at the point on the dial where they'd picked up the Grunians before they could get nothing at all. Further round the dial they did get a sort of rushing sound but after waiting for a minute or so in the hope of some signal coming through they gave it up.

'Now *why* can't we get Grunia?' David puzzled. 'We got it before.'

Toby said: 'When we picked them up we were at home. Perhaps from home you can listen-in only to people talking over here, so . . .'

'So what?'

'So now we're *here*, perhaps we can listen to people talking somewhere back home. Perhaps that wrong transistor you put in, the red one, makes the set link up those two places only. What d'you think?'

'I wonder. Let's go round the dial again.'

Once again the Grunian wavelength yielded nothing but silence. David continued to turn the dial.

'Here's that rushing noise again,' he said. 'Just like last time. No signal, though.'

'Screw the volume up,' suggested Toby.

The rushing grew to a roaring sound as David adjusted the set.

'I don't think you've got anything there,' said Toby. And at that the roaring ceased altogether.

'It's gone dead,' said David.

But hardly had he spoken than a loud, clear voice came from the transistor set.

'*Walter*!' it called. '*Walter*!'

'That's Mother's voice!' exclaimed David.

'Sssh! Listen!'

'*Breakfast's almost ready, Walter,*' said Mrs. Green. '*Better give those boys a call. It's time they were up.*'

'*All right, dear. Just a moment . . .*' answered Mr. Green.

'David! David!' cried Toby. 'What's going to happen when they find we're not there? How are we going to get back? David! What's happening? Where are you going?' For his brother, who was holding the transistor set, was rapidly sliding away from him!

'I don't know,' David shouted in reply. 'This thing is pulling me and I can't let go. Grab hold of my legs, Toby. *Quick!*'

Toby barely managed to get a grip on David's ankles before they were both lifted from the ground and, rising steeply into the dark sky, they hurtled forward at breathtaking speed.

'D-d-d-don't let go of that transistor!' Toby called.

'As if I would!'

After the first shock of the ascent the boys got used to the motion and began almost to enjoy the flight. David said suddenly:

'Toby! There's a car coming towards us!'

'What?!'

'A car. A motor-car!'

'Oh yeah! Perhaps it's the Flying Squad,' said Toby sarcastically.

'But I tell you it is. I can see the headlights.'

And sure enough there were two yellow lamps coming towards them at a tremendous speed.

'We're going to crash!' shouted David.

But at the last moment the twin lamps swerved to one side and a moment later the owl, yellow eyes glowing, had hooked his claws in the collar of David's jacket.

'So Hildrok's gone,' he said.

'Hello, Owl. How do you know?' asked Toby.

'Hawk saw you returning alone,' said the owl. 'But I'm here to bring a message from Captain Cobwebb. He says thank you for all you've done. He'd planned a welcome for you at the Council of Creatures but it seems you're wanted back home rather urgently so the Captain says he'll do his best to get you there as soon as possible. Bless my soul,' added the owl, 'you'll blow my feathers off at this speed. I'll have to let go. Goodbye . . . Goodbye.'

'Goodbye, Owl,' they called and Toby, turning his head, had a brief glimpse of the owl's shining eyes in the darkness behind them before he was lost to sight.

David and Toby swept on through the night and there was nothing but blackness below until, suddenly, David pointed out a glowing circle of light. At that moment they began a steep dive.

The circle below widened into a great bowl of light.

'That's the Council of Creatures,' called David. 'Look, all the animals are there, Toby. See that big desk and that tall, empty chair? That's Uncle Septimus' chair and I expect he's sitting there watching us. And under that big tree there—see, Toby, that's the tunnel I came out of when the parrot brought me from Gallows Peak Farm.'

Down and down they went. The cries of welcome from the animals grew even louder. Now the boys were swooping low, over the chair of Uncle Septimus Cobwebb. And as they did so they heard his deep, laughing voice so close that it seemed as if he were in the air with them.

'Well done, boys!' said Captain Cobwebb. 'I'm proud of you, and all the animals thank you for what you've done for them. Now hold tight . . .'

As he spoke David and Toby saw the black tunnel under the great tree looming up in front of them and they plunged into darkness.

'*Whoossh*!' they went along the tunnel.

'*Bump*!' they went into some obstacles that gave way before them.

And then, after a sudden dizzy spin, '*Bump*! . . .*Bump*!' And there they were, sitting on the floor of their bedroom at home and rubbing their eyes in the bright sunlight.

David looked around for the transistor set. It lay beside him. The case had sprung open but everything inside seemed to be in place. Everything, that was, except the red transistor. In its place there was a green one, just as the instructions said there should be. But before David could call Toby's attention to this curious business, they heard a voice from downstairs.

'Come on, you two,' called Mr. Green. 'You're late and your bacon's getting cold.'

'Coming!' David shouted. He looked at Toby and Toby looked at him. There they were, dressed in jacket and jeans, just as they had been before they set off for

Gallows Peak Farm and their capture by the Wurgs so long ago.

Downstairs they tucked in to their breakfast and they paused only for a moment when, with Mrs. Green in the kitchen and Mr. Green having gone to the door to answer the postman's knock, Toby said:

'Doesn't it all seem like a dream now, David?'

But before David could answer, Mr. and Mrs. Green came into the room. Mr. Green was laughing.

'Poor old Farmer Jenkins!' he said. 'Postman tells me he ran his new car into a ditch last night.'

'Surely that's nothing to laugh at, Walter,' rebuked Mrs. Green.

'Ah, but just listen to the reason *why* he landed up in the ditch. He says that a boy, riding on a fish, went right across the road in front of him. *A boy*, my dear, *riding on a fish*! I ask you!'

'Nobody's going to believe *that*!' said Mrs. Green.